DIMA WANNOUS

The Frightened Ones

TRANSLATED FROM THE ARABIC BY
Elisabeth Jaquette

VINTAGE

1 3 5 7 9 10 8 6 4 2

Vintage is part of the Penguin Random House group of companies
whose addresses can be found at global.penguinrandomhouse.com

First published in Vintage in 2021
First published by Harvill Secker in 2020
First published in Arabic by Dar al-Adab in 2017

penguin.co.uk/vintage

A CIP catalogue record for this book is available from the
British Library

ISBN 9781784707996

This book has been selected to receive financial assistance from
English PEN's 'PEN Translates' programme, supported by Arts
Council England. English PEN exists to promote literature and our
understanding of it, to uphold writers' freedoms around the world,
to campaign against the persecution and imprisonment of writers
for stating their views, and to promote the friendly co-operation of
writers and the free exchange of ideas. www.englishpen.org

Printed and bound in Great Britain by Clays Ltd, Elcograf S.p.A.

The authorised representative in the EEA is Penguin Random House
Ireland, Morrison Chambers, 32 Nassau Street, Dublin D02 YH68.

Penguin Random House is committed to a sustainable future for
our business, our readers and our planet. This book is made from
Forest Stewardship Council® certified paper.

For Ibrahim

Exactly fifteen years ago I was sitting in Kamil's office.

(Kamil, are you reading this now? Does the number fifteen ring a bell? Fifteen years, Kamil – most people would say *all these years*. Though you, in my dreams, talk about just four and a half years as *all these years* . . .)

I was sitting in Kamil's really tiny waiting room, which stretched and swelled to fit dozens of patients. A few people came for appointments they'd made weeks before, or even earlier, but most came from outside Damascus without having booked. They sat on chairs scattered around the room and spilled onto the narrow steps outside. I smoked and watched them. The secretary, Leila, who was unusually sweet, was reading some lectures she'd printed out, studying diligently for her exams. Every so often, she'd steal a glance at me and smile.

Leila. She probably had things on her mind, even while she was so kind to everyone: a person can be both troubled and sweet. She was young, working her way through college, supporting her family, which suffered like so many others. When Leila's father died, her mother came down with all kinds of health problems. She'd been an active woman, and pretty, flitting through life with her svelte fifty-something body. Then her husband passed away and she began to suffer from high blood pressure, diabetes, kidney disease and hypothyroidism. She became a limp, bedridden thing. Leila's divorcée sister and her two-year-old daughter lived with them; there was also a brother, but he had lost his mind years earlier.

What had happened was that at the age of twenty-one he fell in love with a student at the College of Fine Arts. (That's where I'd studied too.) The girl he admired was the daughter of a low-ranking officer from the Mezzeh 86 neighbourhood. One day another boy, whose father was an intelligence officer, happened to see this same girl at college. Leila didn't tell me which agency the father worked for, that part wasn't important: the point was that the boy fell for her too, and wanted to take her on a date to his father's 'rest stop'. (That's what kids of government officials call the gardens on the edge of Damascus reserved for high-ranking officers. Somewhere they can go in their free time, and spend days off with their families.) She turned him down: by this point she and Leila's brother were dating. Then one morning Leila's brother was kidnapped in the street. He disappeared for a whole week and returned an empty shell. 'They hung him from his feet for days, left him upside down, until his mind poured out, to the last drop,' she told me. I remember the phrase too well. Leila told me all this one time when no one was in the waiting room except us. She said her brother came back without his mind. From then on, he shut himself in his room. He'd sit next to the open window, looking out onto the crowded street in Masaken Barzeh and yelling at people. 'Have you seen Hafez al-Assad?' he'd ask them. 'If you see him, tell him I won't leave my room until he comes to visit in person.' No one paid any attention. Crazy. Lost his mind. He'd urinate out the window and point his penis directly at whoever was passing, oblivious to their insults or swearing.

Leila spent her days in that tiny waiting room, around people not dissimilar to her brother in one way or another. They had stories just as strange as his. She studied, scheduled appointments, drank Nescafé with milk and smoked voraciously. Then she went home to care for her weak, bedridden mother, her divorced only sister, her niece, and her brother, who was a prisoner to his room and his madness. I often watched Leila and considered her sweet disposition, which radiated from her eyes, despite everything around her. I imagined how hard it must be for someone to act as mother, father, doctor and husband, and keep it all together. You'd think that their expression would show the strain of what they have to carry,

3

crushed one minute, resilient the next. That their eyes might glaze over callously, then glow with sudden tenderness. But not Leila.

I sat scanning each of the people in the waiting room. A young man in his early thirties arrived. Tall. Broad shoulders. Strong features, as if they'd been drawn or even sculpted on his face. Thick hair, jet black. He had a broad chest, and I envied him his ribcage, that it could expand to hold so much air. (I didn't feel real jealousy then, not in that first brief encounter. That feeling wouldn't come until we'd got to know each other better.) You see, I was desperately afraid of suffocating, terrified by the thought of the air around me running out. Unable to take in any more, I'd die of asphyxiation while this man watched and took deep breaths to fill his own lungs, which were more spacious than those of ordinary people. Our ribcages have atrophied. Even at their best, they arch no further than our stomachs.

I didn't particularly notice his muscles that day, how firm, sinuous and prominent they were. (When he flexed, you could see that he was obsessed with each one individually, that he'd worked to develop each muscle in isolation. That first day, most of this remained hidden under his heavy winter clothes.) But at one point he rolled up his sleeves and bared his forearms, and when I glanced down at them, they were so solid. I'm crazy about the area between the wrist and the elbow. That short stretch of skin sends me somewhere so expansive

4

there's always enough space, and enough oxygen. I'm enamoured of bones. Especially a body with prominent bones. I'm never drawn to people whose bones are hidden beneath soft flesh: I hunt for bulges on hands, wrists and throats, the base of the neck, the collarbone – the collarbone? How can such an unwieldy word invoke such a warm, tender spot?

When he sat down and bared his forearms I saw the contours of his wrist bones, under soft skin lightly covered with black hair. I dropped my gaze to his feet. Jeans, hitched up a bit because he'd crossed one leg over the other. Between the top of one trainer and the bottom of his jeans another bone budded. There was no clear or rational explanation for my obsession with bones. (I didn't tell Kamil that I love bones more than anything else.)

This man and all his bones sat in a metal chair covered with cheap brown leather. I looked at him. He didn't notice me. To be fair, he didn't seem to notice anyone. He lit a cigarette and went to ash it on the ground; Leila glanced at him, surprised.

'There's an ashtray on the table in front of you,' she said softly, cutting through the reverie he was drowning in. (Thoughts as deep as the sea, the sea I later learned he feared.)

His eyes widened but he didn't apologise. He just looked to the left, at the chipped ashtray, and stubbed out his cigarette, ignoring the ashes he'd purposefully let fall. He didn't bend down to clean the floor but behaved as if he were on the street or in the park, where sooner or later a breeze would come to do the job. As if Leila weren't there. He didn't seem to consider that she'd be the one to sweep up his mess a few minutes later.

I went in for my appointment with Kamil. The whole time I spoke with him, it felt as if the man in the waiting room were listening to my life flowing out onto the pages of the little notebook on Kamil's desk, where he recorded his incomprehensible symbols. I felt a heavy sadness that day. I'd planned to tell Kamil about a strange dream from the night before, but I changed my mind. (Was the stranger with prominent bones, sitting on the other side of the thin wooden door, the reason why?) I didn't tell Kamil that in my dream I'd been sitting on the roof of an old low building in Damascus. The moon was full. I sat on the edge, and wasn't worried about falling. I looked at the moon and was glad it was full, which surprised me, because I don't usually like the full moon. I don't like things that are round, finished or whole. I like things lacking: absence makes me feel complete. But that night, in my dream, I was glad about the full harvest moon, round as a piece of flatbread. It was whole, my soul was whole; the moon felt like a mirror, reflecting how full and complete I am. (I usually punish myself obsessively for mistakes I may or may not have made, blame myself for things that are wrong with the world, hold myself partially responsible. Maybe just because I exist? Does my simple presence in this strange time make me responsible for some of its catastrophes?) Then, suddenly, in my dream, my heart dropped. Why would it not? The moon fell to the earth and I felt my heart tumble down with it. The loss was painful. Palpable. I saw a VW Beetle driving through the sky. Without the moon, the night was so dark. A man was at the wheel, and his wife was sitting next to him. I didn't know for sure she was his wife, but the resignation on her face made me think so. Do all married people look so resigned? The man driving his car through the sky was in his sixties, and his wife was about the same. But I didn't tell Kamil about my dream. I fumbled and lost the desire to speak. Kamil pressed me, questioned me, tried to tease words from my mouth, and all the while I thought about the man sitting outside. As I left Kamil's office, I looked the man in the eye. He was lost in thought. He looked at me, but absently, as if he saw the waiting-room door open and close but not anyone walking through it.

Several weeks after that brief encounter, I saw him in the waiting room again. His appointment was right before mine. When he left, I went in. After I was done, I said goodbye to Leila and went down the long narrow staircase. I was surprised to see him sitting on the front step of the building. As I passed, I said hello. He looked at me with that same vague expression.

'I've been waiting for you for fifty minutes,' he said. 'Do you want to get a cup of coffee?'

I nodded.

We walked together, in no particular direction and without saying a word, all the way to Hamra Street, then to Shalaan, and then to the Cham Palace Hotel, where he paused and entered without asking if I would rather go there or somewhere else. I followed him in. He chose the table next to the window, and I sat down across from him.

He called the waiter over and said without hesitation, 'Bring me a beer – an Almaza, really cold.' He didn't ask what I wanted to drink.

The waiter glanced at me expectantly. 'A cup of coffee,' I said.

The man hadn't looked at me yet: he'd been busy staring at people walking by outside. I felt uneasy. *What am I doing here with this strange man with prominent bones?* I wondered. I didn't even know his name and it felt strange to ask. How had I agreed to go out with a man whose name I didn't know? He hadn't asked mine either – maybe he didn't care.

He lit a cigarette. He had an odd way of smoking. He took a deep drag, exhaled a breath of smoke, and then sucked it in again. I stared at the smoke he was breathing out and in: he didn't lose a single puff. He seemed confident in his solid, firm body, as if he were dense and filled with his self, the way I felt in the dream I hadn't mentioned to Kamil. I wondered why he was seeing Kamil. Was it to build this self-confidence? Had Kamil made him the person he was now? He raised his glass to his lips and drank with an air of purpose. This made him seem even more confident. I sipped my lukewarm coffee; the taste made me queasy. I felt tension rise to my head. Cold sweat beaded my face. My heartbeat began its dreaded gallop, pounding my chest, through my veins, up my neck; I snapped open my purse and began searching frantically for the bottle of Xanax. I broke off half a tablet and placed it under my tongue, the way Kamil had advised me to do when I had intense flashes of anxiety. The tablet, or rather half of it, dissolved and I took a sip of water.

The man whose name I still didn't know noticed what I was doing. He saw me frantically reach into my purse, pull out a bottle, swallow half a tablet of something he didn't recognise and take a sip of water. He looked at me. He fixed his gaze on me with his usual calm, though back then, fifteen years ago, I wasn't used to his composure. His expression didn't change at all. It didn't contract or expand; he wasn't surprised, or curious about my sudden panic. That made the half a Xanax work faster. (When I feel like that, questions only increase my unease: having to explain, to justify, to respond, feels absurd and further heightens my anxiety.) The man downed the last drop of beer and asked for the check, paid the bill and abruptly stood.

'Thanks for coming out with me,' he said. 'I'm sure we'll see each other again. Glad to have met you.'

And then he left, as if he'd never been there at all.

I wondered why he was *sure we'd see each other again*. What made him so certain? And he was glad to have met me! Could he really say we'd met? We hadn't even spoken. He drank his beer and I sipped my warmish, nauseating coffee, and then he went. Did he mean we'd sit together again, drinking beer and coffee? Did he miss having someone next to him while he finished a beer?

A few weeks later, it did all happen again. I left Kamil's office and found the man sitting on the front steps, smoking. 'Coffee?' he asked. I thought about how he'd invited me for a cup of coffee and then ordered a beer. He'd abridged his invitation this time, an enquiry with a question mark suspended in the air. I could see it flying around his head, attached to a string of letters jumbled on top of each other, obscuring one another. I nodded, agreeing reluctantly, and started walking; he followed me. Almost immediately I stopped.

'I don't like the café at the Cham Palace Hotel,' I told him.

'Where would you rather go?' he asked.

'The Marmar,' I said swiftly.

He turned to me without missing a beat and before I could even begin to back-pedal he said, 'OK.'

I don't know why I suggested a bar. Was it to be clear from the start? Was it because he had invited me for coffee again, even though he planned on ordering beer? The Marmar was no place for a coffee.

So there we were, standing on the kerb in front of

Kamil's office. It was a little after seven. Women wandered past with children in tow, and street vendors spread their Chinese wares down the long pavement in al-Jisr al-Abyad. The commotion made me anxious and I hurried to stop a taxi. There was a lot of traffic, so I walked a few metres in search of an empty cab while he waited. Several minutes passed before we found one. I got in the back seat and he climbed in next to me: I thought that was weird. (Usually, men sit up front, next to the driver. For him to sit in the back, with me, was something most taxi drivers frown at. They take it as an insult to their masculinity, or at the very least they see it as a slight to the passenger's masculinity for him to sit in the back next to a woman.) Neither of us moved so I told the driver, 'Bab Touma, please,' and the man whose name I still didn't know slipped his hand into mine. He held my hand and gazed out the window, disinterestedly, not even caring to look into my eyes. All I could think of was how much I liked his hands. His lovely fingers were holding mine, and I tried not to ruin the moment but surrendered my hand to his; he grasped it firmly, so it wouldn't slip away. His hand was warm. Mine was cold, making his seem even warmer by comparison. Was his heart cold? (My mother always says, 'Cold hands, warm heart.' I've never heard her say the reverse.)

I didn't tell Leila that we went out several times. I don't think he told her either; he didn't have a good relationship with her in any case, not since he had ashed his cigarette on the floor. He never asked me why I was seeing Kamil. And I didn't ask him. We went out once a month at first, then every two weeks, and eventually not a week went by without us meeting up at least once. I learned his name: Naseem. I found out he was a writer, too. I searched all the bookshops I knew and even the ones I didn't for the books he'd written, but I couldn't find a single one. Even the keenest booksellers hadn't heard of him, and in those days you couldn't search for something on Google. Our lives were closed; it was incredibly boring. I told Naseem I couldn't find any of his books, and he smiled. (It wasn't easy to make him smile, not at all: his lips parted with effort, self-consciously, and he didn't relax until he'd closed them.) Later, I found out that his books were published under a pseudonym.

'Afraid of being harassed?' I asked. He shook his head.

'Afraid of fear.' A pause. He didn't say more.

I felt an overwhelming urge to hug him, to embrace the strange man sitting across from me, about whom I still knew practically nothing, just that he had prominent bones and wrote under a pseudonym.

I knew my encounters with this man and his bones were changing me. *Afraid of fear.* This phrase was the deep current beneath my life: fear doesn't have just one form; fear of fear never leaves you.

I asked him to describe what he meant by being afraid of fear. 'Writers are probably better at explaining things than anyone else,' I said. 'Is it normal for fear to make someone lose their ability to imagine?'

'Exactly. Fear ruins the imagination.'

That's all he would say.

Naseem was afraid of fear. Not the fear of being detained, prosecuted, interrogated or prevented from leaving the country, but a fear that came before all those other fears. Since Naseem was afraid of living in fear, he pre-empted it by writing under a pseudonym. This protected him, in a way. I thought more about what he'd said, and realised he wasn't just afraid of being afraid after the book was published, but also while writing. If he wrote under his own name that fear would inevitably influence his work. Under a pseudonym, he could write more openly. He was free of self-censorship; he could be braver.

Under his real name, Naseem wasn't an author, he was a doctor. Why didn't he just say he was a doctor, instead of introducing himself as a writer without telling me his pen name? I didn't ask if he'd ever thought about the owner of the publishing house, whether they might be forced to reveal their author's true identity? I didn't ask: I was afraid of fear. Afraid of frightening him.

I was holding my mobile in my right hand, pressing it hard against my ear. With my left hand, I massaged my right shoulder, then held my index finger against the large vein on the left side of my neck. I felt my heartbeats gallop, racing one after another. I was frightened. My lips went numb, my forehead felt cold and a glassy layer of sweat formed under my nose. I couldn't hear my heart, I couldn't understand what it was saying. What I heard was a voice reciting something; I saw each sentence swirling as a strange string of letters. More letters piled up and were quickly lost, obscured by the shadows of other letters. Among them I could make out the first two letters of the alphabet: *'alif, bā'* ... I saw Naseem riding the *bā'* with its low curve, then holding on to the straight vertical line of the *'alif,* while the *hamza* floated above his head like a hat.

(This image had been with me every time we'd met. I'd sit across from him and stare at the hamza suspended over his head; he probably thought I was staring off into space. He would seem disinterested, though maybe he was used to me staring at nothing in particular. As we got closer, I often held my gaze there: at nothingness. At anything except for his eyes, which I came to know so well. When you know someone well, when you've heard everything they have to say and nothing surprises you, you stop looking. Instead, you search through the emptiness for somewhere you can take refuge; anywhere aside from those painfully kind eyes.)

When the voice in my head finally stopped, the string of flying letters linked like a train – like a toy you might use to teach children how to read – faded away. They vanished, replaced by the harsh sound of a slap. Naseem. I'd know from the start that our call would end with a slap. I fell silent for several seconds, or maybe just one second, it didn't matter. It started with a slap to his face: he began fiercely slapping his right cheek with his right hand; I heard the sound of his fingers striking his skin and saw, or imagined, it going red; saw how his cheek glowed between the fine hairs of his beard and how the line he'd carefully shaved grew less distinct against the marks of his five fingers. He hit himself with all five fingers, the whole hand, to feel content, to feel pain. Pleasure is the moment that pain subsides, he told me once. Was that why he was doing this? Was he hitting himself to feel pain, and then pleasure when the pain passed? Or was he giving himself a slap in the face? (An Iraqi friend of mine from the College of Fine Arts used to call an insulting situation 'a slap in the face'. Was this what she meant? I imagined her doing the slapping.)

I kept quiet because I didn't know how to stop him: I've never known what to do in crazy situations like this. I get confused. It's not that I'm afraid; I just get confused and freeze up. Then the call dropped, just like it always did. I heard nothing. I thought about my hands. I've never hit myself. I have used them to give myself a hug, not something I do often, and I can't remember the last time, but I wrap my arms around my body until my fingers brush the sides of my back. I hug myself, run my fingers through my hair and whisper, 'Don't be afraid, darling. Take a deep breath, nice and slow. Don't be afraid, *habibti*. It's just another panic attack. You'll get through it. Breathe.'

A dream. I was driving a car. The road was going uphill; I didn't know where it was leading. Though I couldn't feel my body, I was also sitting in the passenger seat, next to myself in the driver's seat, occasionally casting sidelong glances at myself. The me sitting next to me wasn't anxious at all. But the me that was driving the car up the hill was dying of fear and anxiety. On the other side of the road, the ocean stretched as far as I could see. The wind was raging. (I hate the wind. I can handle the cold, no matter how bitter it is, and torrential rains too; I can be soaked and still delight in the downpour. But I hate the wind. I'm afraid of the sound it makes. When it roars, my soul heaves, and I feel as if it's going to throw me off balance or knock me down. Even when I'm at home and able to hide, the sound terrifies me.) I was driving up the hill and the wind was raging, dumping buckets of seawater onto the road where I was driving with myself. I had to hurry and reach the summit: my house was there. I didn't know if it was actually my house, but it was a house I was steadily approaching. My heart began pounding as we drove further, and this surprised me; it wasn't as if I was running uphill. All I had to do was press the gas pedal with my toes for the car to accelerate. But my heart insisted on galloping; I felt it was about to explode. I glanced across out of the corner of my eye and saw myself gazing calmly, indifferently out at the sea battering itself on us, as if my other self were sitting on the beach enjoying the warm May sunshine, among families laughing and delighting in the arrival of summer. Meanwhile, I was racing uphill before the sea swallowed us whole. (In reality, I am not actually afraid of the sea. Water doesn't terrify me. I am a good swimmer, skilled at navigating the current and letting my body drift with the motion of the waves. It is Naseem who fears the sea. He will only swim parallel to the shore and he told me he would drown if his feet couldn't touch the sand. It has nothing to do with his swimming ability; he too is a good swimmer. But as soon as he goes into the water and lets it cover his body, he becomes as heavy as a stone. He feels too weighty to move, and flounders.) But Naseem wasn't with me as I drove up the hill and as my heart pounded in terror. Sweat poured from my body, as if it were a sponge left to soak and then wrung out all at once. Naseem, who was afraid of the ocean, wasn't with me. I was with myself. What did that mean? Was Naseem the fear that made sweat stream from my skin, his spirit nestled in mine, inside me? In the depth of my imagination and the folds of my memories, ones I had experienced and ones I had yet to create? Why was I so afraid? Then suddenly, as if to explain, we were somewhere else. I don't know where exactly. Somewhere that looked like an airport. I do have all sorts of fears associated with crowds and people running with their bags, out of breath. Planes, flying, crashes, death. But this time I wasn't scared. It was as if I'd borrowed Naseem's fears of the sea, water and drowning and now, in the airport, I was rid of my own. I swapped my fear of the sky for his fear of the earth, or at least the parts of the earth that were covered by water.

I was sitting at a large table. Naseem was sitting far away. And next to me, as if by chance, sat Kamil, drinking a coffee and smoking a cigarette. I didn't ask how he dared to smoke in an airport. I wasn't surprised to see him next to me, didn't ask how he got there. He looked at me the way he always did, from behind a cloud of smoke billowing from his mouth and nose. He began chastising me. Said I hadn't changed in all these years. Whether sitting, standing, speaking, eating, drinking, smoking or thinking, I was still the way I'd always been. Hadn't budged an inch. This annoyed me – why had he come to chastise me and make me doubt myself, after all these years? (I borrowed his phrase, *all these years*. Even though it has only been four and a half, not ages, just a few months in a neat little stack. Though perhaps they really are *all these years*, because how could anyone comprehend everything we've experienced in just four and a half? Impossible.)

'What have you done with your fear, after all these years?' he asked me.

'Fear matures with us,' I told him. He looked into my eyes with that steady gaze of his, the one that seemed to well up from his soul.

'Fear doesn't mature with us.' His words emerged from lips hidden behind a thick moustache. 'But it can stay with us our whole lives. What have you done to make fear cling to your soul?'

'It doesn't cling to my soul,' I objected.

'No?' he asked, his gentle smile laced with something mean. 'I see it streaming from your eyes, pouring right out of them.'

As he said this, I felt a sharp wind lash across my face. I shut my eyes and wished that when I opened them it would all be over, but I knew nothing stopped that easily. I opened my eyes . . . and everything was the same. Kamil, and Naseem, and the place that looked like a stuffy, grimy airport. I was the same, too, unafraid. Even though I was

20

in an airport, I was calm. (It's a terrible paradox: you have to be afraid to observe your fears and monitor them carefully. You try to push them away, to grab them like a handful of leaves and throw them far from you. But leaves are light. So then you try to grab your fears like a handful of stones and throw them far away, and they do land far away, they're no longer stuck to you, or even near you, like the weightless green leaves were.)

Then I saw Naseem walk off without me. It must have been time to board the plane. I didn't call out to him, I didn't shout. No. I stood up, perfectly calm, said goodbye to Kamil, and slowly walked in the direction that Naseem had taken. He'd vanished behind a throng of quickly moving people with bags. Then I glanced to my left and saw a friend of my father's, Elias, exiting a room made of wood. Elias and my father worked together at the Italian Hospital. I went up to him and noticed blood dripping from his left nostril. He put his finger in his nose, trying to staunch the flow, and said, almost begging, 'Please, Antoinette, do catch up.' I didn't know who Antoinette was. Then, someone who must have been Antoinette emerged from the room wearing white clothes and white shoes, like the ones nurses wear. She caught up with him and eased him into a long, metal, coffin-like box. As soon as she laid him down, blood began pouring from every part of his body, the way sweat streamed from mine as I drove up the hill. Elias was close to drowning in the hot blood spilling from his arteries, bright as a chrysanthemum. To his left, stretched out in a long metal box like the one in which he lay, was a man I didn't know. His head and face were half open. His eyes were detached, but he could still see. He stared into my eyes, pleading for help. I stood there, unable to do anything. It wasn't like I felt frozen, as happens sometimes in dreams when you try to move and realise you can't. No, I was completely powerless. I tried to take a step closer and my feet were there, but I couldn't make myself move. I looked down at his head. It was cracked down the middle, split open, and filled with onions. Peeled, boiled onions of all different sizes. I'm not sure how I knew they were boiled, I just did. Maybe I could tell by their shape or colour. I don't know. Fresh or boiled, it didn't matter. I left the two men on the brink of death and ran. I wanted to catch my flight and find Naseem, whose fear of the sea I'd borrowed. I boarded the plane, it lifted off and we circled above the city, flying so close to the ground that people could raise their hands and brush its metal underbelly as we flew by.

I opened my eyes to the soft, dismal light of dawn and wished that I really could borrow Naseem's fear of the sea. I wished I could take his fear in exchange for all of mine. Then I thought about the boiled onions growing out of the strange man's head. Merciless, these dreams. No sooner had I caught my breath from the day than I was out of breath in my dreams.

Again I heard a voice, reciting; I saw each sentence swirling as a strange string of letters. More letters piled up and were quickly lost, obscured by the shadows of other letters. And then they vanished, replaced by the harsh sound of a slap. Why was I living this scene again? I didn't know.

I didn't tell Naseem when we next spoke that I'd dreamed about him, or that he had boarded the plane before me, without waiting for me. Or that for the first time ever I wasn't afraid of airplanes or airports. More importantly, I didn't tell him how I'd borrowed his fear of the sea. When I called him that morning, I didn't tell him that I had rid him of his fears for ever, and so he shouldn't worry. Did he keep slapping his face after the end of the call? Did he cry? (No, Naseem doesn't cry. He says that men don't cry. I don't tell him that crying isn't the only thing that traditionally men aren't allowed to do; they are not allowed to feel afraid, either. I'm not just talking about the fear of drowning, I mean more complex fears.) Naseem didn't let himself cry. Tears welled up, his eyelids grew round and his eyes gleamed, but he didn't let the tears fall; they receded. He swallowed them: his eyes could swallow the way his throat did. The way, when I was little, my mother told me, 'Zip it and swallow them . . . swallow them.' She forbade me from crying by telling me to swallow my tears. I wondered if Naseem was afraid of drowning in his tears. Had his fear of water grown that bad? So bad he'd stop himself from crying, afraid his tears might pour out, submerge him and leave him splashing around, unable to breathe?

I said none of this to him.

He'd sent me the manuscript for his fourth novel, the one I thought he'd already finished. I still had never been able to read any of his previous books. I inhaled this one word after word, letter by letter, drinking in commas and devouring full stops. And as I did, I realised that it was unfinished, not as a novel should be: it was more like a memoir, about a woman shaped by fear. Like me. Like him.

What did Naseem want? Did he want me to write the ending? Had he started the novel, only to be consumed by fear? Did he not have the strength to finish it? Didn't Naseem know that absence makes me feel complete? Did he think that if I completed his novel for him, I would feel complete, the way I had the night years ago when I dreamed I was sitting on the roof of a low old building in Damascus, dangling my feet off the edge, the full moon in my heart? I hadn't told Kamil about that dream at the time; I'd been distracted by the man with the prominent bones sitting on the other side of the wooden door. Was it a coincidence that we met just hours after I saw the moon fall from the sky? The moon was full that night, and I'd felt complete, but this novel, it lacked an ending.

Naseem's manuscript

I remember our living room well. I remember our carpet, green with dark green embroidery, and how I often rolled it out to play. The only thing that cut the silence was the creak and chirp of the wooden shutters. I lived my childhood in silence, so much so that when I summon the few scenes I do recall to memory, they appear without sound. They're silent. No commotion. No voices. No music. Just windows chirping.

The electricity often went in our building for days at a time. Those across the way would still be lit, while we alone were drowning in darkness. Our power lines were connected to the close-knit neighbourhood of Esh al-Warwar, some distance away, where most residents were from Alawite officer families. When they experienced power cuts, so did we, and ours would be the only building in our neighbourhood to go dark, right in the middle of all the others. I remember the first telephone number I memorised: the emergency number for the power company. They rarely answered the phone, and sometimes left it off the hook intentionally for hours.

These frequent dark spells were one reason for the depression that began to settle over me. Another was that home meant illness. In the kitchen, my mother kept odd-looking herbs and plants with foreign names like alfalfa, aloe and nettle, which she washed, chopped and juiced for my father to drink. He did not like the taste and complained about his wife's natural recipes, but he hoped they would boost his immune system and return the colour to his face. My father lay in bed for hours, reading or writing. When he tired of this, he moved from his room to the sitting room and listened to the radio or a record of Fairuz, Vivaldi, Bach or Jacques Brel. At home, I was his shadow. But a very still shadow, one that hardly moved. All I remember doing as a child was sticking to his side. Watching him, listening to him breathe. Catching his gaze and trying to decipher it. I knew him so well that often I knew what he was going to say before he said it. It wasn't hard: we shared the same thoughts, as if by a secret pact. We were exhaustingly candid. Held nothing back. There were no limits to our thinking, nothing forbidden, no right or wrong. No absolutes. Everything was open to discussion, often endlessly and extensively so. I was expected to speak and listen, and this made me ask more of life. I was insatiable, always seeking more: I had no time for endings, and knew nothing more beautiful than beginnings. Things never ended, they only began, and as soon as we discovered one beginning, we started searching for the next. Locks were forbidden, and naturally keys as well. Secrets, too, because we trusted each other. Shame was forbidden. We dressed and undressed with the doors open, because we were not embarrassed by our bodies. What could there be to be embarrassed about?

Home for me was my father's bedroom, where I spent most of my time sitting on the edge of his bed or lying next to it. Home was also the door to the little kitchen balcony, where I spied on taxis, wondering which one held my mother inside. She was often gone for hours at a time, going from doctors' clinics to labs to al-Buzuriyah market, to buy anything that might strengthen his immune system: almonds, walnuts, local honey, royal jelly, bee pollen, cactus innards, apricot kernels . . . It put my mother at ease to know my father was not alone in the house. But when she was late returning, fear stirred in my chest. I would stand at the balcony door waiting for her to come home, my eyes trained on taxis while my ears remained pricked, ready to catch my father's voice if he called. Even when he called for me, he whispered my name, as if I were sitting right next to him.

In later years, my father spent most of the afternoon sleeping. Whenever my mother was out, I spent the whole time walking on tiptoe between the kitchen and his room. I would stand outside his door and wait until my pupils widened and my eyes grew accustomed to the dark. Then I would feel my way forward, step by step, afraid of bumping into the bed or dresser and waking him. I would come closer. Bend over him. My long hair was always kept braided or tied back. He was always lying there, sleeping on his side, and I would draw closer and try to hear him breathing. When I could not, I reached a finger towards him, slowly, so incredibly slowly I felt frozen with concentration. All of my senses were condensed into the tip of my finger stretching towards him. I got closer and closer, ever so cautiously, so as not to touch his lips or nose and wake him. When I felt warm air brush the tip of my finger, I relaxed ... he was breathing.

One afternoon, he called for me. His face was pale. He asked for a cup of coffee, the one thing in our dreary home I could make proficiently. I remember our little coffeepot well, too; it was made of thick, dark steel. Its colour never dulled, because my mother was obsessive about cleaning and forbade the natural progression of things. She soaked the pot from time to time in boiling water, salt and lemon juice, and the steel was rejuvenated and reclaimed its natural shine. I opened the filtered-water tap and filled the coffeepot just over halfway, then added the coffee grounds. I lit the stove, placed the pot on the hob and watched it heat up as if nothing existed but that small circle of water. My life was full, just like the coffeepot. I stood there, and grew tired of standing. I watched the water, knowing that what Baba really wanted was for us to talk about something. Coffee was just an entry to conversation. My stomach clenched. Talking was agony, but a cup of coffee was a stepping stone. A susurrus of steam interrupted my thoughts. A spoonful of sugar, the brew foamed, then calmed. Three spoonfuls of coffee, and it foamed again. The coffee rose and foamed and then fell. I loved that viscous foam, it reminded me of hot milk mixed with Turkish coffee. (When I was young, we did not yet have Nescafé: we used to drink hot Turkish coffee with milk, and it was delicious. The taste is still sharp in my mind.) I brought the coffee to a boil until all trace of foam had disappeared. I placed the pot on a small tray alongside a caramel-coloured cup, its thick sides decorated with olive flowers. I lifted the tray, always walking slowly so the coffee would not spill. In those days I wore clogs, and my mother had shown me how to move in them as easily as if I were barefoot. I walked through the house like a ghost, no footfall preceding me. (With daily practice, the nerves in my toes and feet grew used to constricting clogs, slippers and all kinds of shoes, even heels. The sound of skidding on tiles was never heard in our house.)

I entered his room. He did not look pale any more. His bed was on the right side. (Every six months my mother rearranged the position of their beds: sometimes she slept in the left bed, and other times in the right one . . . that was how it went.) The bed on the right was grey, and its wooden headboard was decorated with carved flowers and leaves. My father was sitting up, leaning against a pillow with the quilt pulled up to his chest. I poured a coffee for him and placed it on the nightstand to his right, and he asked me to sit next to him. He gave me a tender smile to start the conversation. Then he uttered a single sentence, in a voice firm and composed: 'The doctor in Paris told me I only have three months to live – we still have three months together.' I could not contain my feelings in that moment. A pang passed through me, and my eyes filled silently with tears. I remember my voice disappeared, and my body began to tremble. My eyes swam and all I could see was darkness; the tears gathered under my eyelids and then streamed down, and I remember feeling their heat on my face. I could not move. At the time, I did not know how this moment would change my life, that the trembling would stay with me and remain part of me until this day. My father opened his arms to hug me and in one movement I went towards him, as if I were a statue being lifted from one place to another. I flung myself onto his chest. An anguished sob crept up through my lungs and escaped; I could not swallow it. I kissed his neck like I always did. I loved his neck. Even now, I can still almost feel his skin against my lips. That spot on his neck was home for me. It made me feel safe and secure. I let my head fall on his shoulders, pressed my face into the wall of his neck and peacefully dozed off. I never found the spot again after that.

I don't know how I got here. Am I intentionally defying Kamil's advice not to keep a journal? Or am I indulging a fundamental need for escape, even if just momentarily? Those long, cruel years still unsettle my sense of security; they have never released their grip on my life. What else did Kamil say that evening? That my life is not substantial enough to write a journal about. He tried to coax me out of silence after that, but I had little interest in speaking. So he tried to lead me towards happier memories. After all, my childhood had not been entirely terrible, and the hellish parts must have receded at times in my early years. But happiness, if it existed, had not imprinted itself in my memory. Happiness was fragile, faint and elusive, no more than a glimmer in the looming sadness. And sadness was all that remained; it bore down on me with all its weight, cast an impossibly long shadow, and completely filled the space where other feelings might have grown. It made me feel as if I had never known anything else.

Then Kamil coaxed out another suppressed memory. I told him my life was filled with women, and my father was the only man. I had my mother, and an aunt on my mother's side I had also called 'Mama' from the time I learned to speak. This aunt had two daughters; one of them married young and had a daughter my age. And there also was an aunt on my father's side, who had three girls and three boys. My grandmother on my mother's side had died when I was young. (I have an image of her once giving me a translucent brown plate piled high with white sugar, which I devoured behind my mother's back. I can still taste it and still hear the granules crunch.) My grandmother on my father's side was still alive. I told Kamil that my childhood was filled with women, and not just any women. Women who were strong, who spoke with confidence. They raised their voices so often the sound still echoed in my memory; these women commanded whole families and managed affairs with aplomb. When it came to men, all I had was my father. My mother's father had passed away when I was quite young, too. All I remember from the later years of his life was him lying in his little bed, on the ground floor of our house in the Afeef neighbourhood in Damascus. He always kept a bag of sweets he called 'caramels' hidden next to him: he snacked on them and often gave me some too. I helped to conceal his sweet tooth, not realising until later that he suffered from diabetes and his legs had been rotting away with gangrene. My paternal grandfather, however, lived until he was quite old, over one hundred, but my relationship with him was tepid and rather complicated. My mother had one brother, but when I was five years old, the taxi he drove flipped over on his way back from Homs. The accident left him paralysed on one side. He was a different person after that, and I lost the young uncle who had been so mild-tempered, full of life and always laughing. My father had an older brother, but there had been a falling-out and I did not meet him until I was twelve. He had another brother whom I adored, but who also died young. This brother had suffered from infantile paralysis and was confined to a bed in a hastily built little room on the roof of a house in the village – a house he actually owned. He spent his days drinking coffee and moonshine, smoking long Alhamra cigarettes and listening to the radio. The room always smelled foul, because the only one who tended to him was his careless sister. She was their middle sibling. I did not really know her, because my father had fallen out with her too. She had rented her paralysed brother's house out to a family in the village, on the condition that they build a room on the roof for him. That was where he lived, drowning in filth, suffering the cold and humidity. This uncle passed away fourteen years ago, after drinking tainted local moonshine.

No men in my life except for my father. The rest were either sick or dead. Kamil nodded, and that strange, changeless smile played upon his lips. The smile lasted for several seconds, and then vanished with a nod. Maybe Kamil's lips were connected to the movement of his head. All he had to do was nod to make his smile disappear, and then he could go back to his papers and questions. 'What about your father's mother?' he asked. I didn't understand the question. What did he want from my relationship with Khadija? How important could my relationship with my grandmother be? She lived in a village far away, and I only saw her on vacations. But Kamil insisted. He wanted to know more about her.

I have never encountered anyone in my life as even-tempered as my grandmother Khadija. She was never cheerful, nor flustered. Her mood was constant and steady, and she was impossible to unsettle. She sometimes got angry, but even that did not change her temperament. She would keep smiling at us, even when annoyed. Her anger never struck randomly; it was always directed at my grandfather. He was the only one who made her cross. No one else. I have never met anyone who talked to herself like my grandmother, either. I constantly heard her chatting to herself in the kitchen while cleaning or doing the washing-up. She told stories I did not understand, using different voices for different characters, and sometimes she also sang folk songs or poems.

My father and I usually took a yellow taxi to the village and arrived in the afternoon. He always sat beside me in the back seat, smoking the whole way there. Every five minutes felt like an hour to me. 'How much longer till we get there?' I would ask, as three and a half hours passed lethargically. My father would gaze out of the window, lost in the road and his cigarette, while I observed the leaning cypress trees as we approached Homs. Seen from our vantage point, the ancient trees seemed shaped by the wild wind. They bent towards Damascus, as I remember. Near the trees, on the other side of the road, there was a rest stop my father loved, though I do not know why. 'Seaside Rest Stop'. We always stopped there on our way to the village, and on our return trip too. I remember loving all the games and toys piled up behind the dusty shop window. Baba always ordered a cup of coffee and continued his cigarette, while I ate a grilled cheese sandwich. I remember how thin it was from the grill, and how the kashkaval cheese dripped down the sides, melted and delicious. We would spend about a quarter of an hour there before continuing on our way.

I loved the second part of our journey. The road from Homs to Tartus was shorter, and more picturesque. The land became greener and the stretches of desert, with their dusty, desolate hue, gradually disappeared. The road began to bend and wind, snaking to the left and right, rising and falling until we reached the outskirts of Tartus. (After my father passed away, I came to love the first part of the journey more than the second. The rocky mountains rising slowly into the distance behind stretches of desert somehow reassured me.) I remember the cement factory that spouted black smoke, poisoning people nearby, and the shadow it cast over ruined olive trees. Rates of cancer had risen in the surrounding area, and in Damascus. Baba was sick with cancer too, as if factory smoke had carried it all the way to his new home, hundreds of kilometres from the village. I remember a statue of Hafez al-Assad, hand raised, greeting everyone coming and going. I remember another statue, too, near Homs: half of a person who appeared to have been sitting. And on the other side of the road, a statue that was life-sized, or even bigger, alone on a hill. I remember the sign as well: 'Smile! You're in Dayr Atiyah'.

My father was strange. I don't mean his personality. It was not that he acted strange, but that he seemed estranged, somehow, from everything around him. He moved through the world as a stranger, at a distance from objects, people, voices and smells. As if the world extended no further than his own body; as if it ended at his tender skin. Silent and decisive, he watched life go by from the taxi window like someone contemplating their fate. His gaze emanated a certain directionless fear. (My father, despite his inner strength and confidence, feared odd little things. He was afraid of chilly weather, for example, and of catching a cold or a sore throat. He was afraid of travel and traffic and stressed out by large crowds. He was afraid I might choke on a piece of food, so he watched me closely whenever I ate. He would open his mouth, and I would open mine for him to place a piece of food inside. He closed his mouth when I closed mine. And slowly chewed while I did too, playing along to please him. He would pretend to swallow and I would see his throat move, then I would swallow my food too. I imagined him digesting the air while I digested my food. Now here I am, often feeling as if I cannot breathe, choking on air, not food. Is it the same air my father closed his mouth around, the same air he swallowed?)

Several years after he passed, a friend of his from Tartus, who was in his mid-fifties and had since moved to Lebanon, gave me a bundle of letters my father had written to him when they were in Year 10 at school. In one, my father wrote of lying awake at night in fear of throat cancer. He was fifteen years old at the time! And it was not until his forties that he was diagnosed with throat cancer. Did he conjure illness from his imagination? Had he lived in fear for all those years? Had he been expecting it?

We always arrived in the afternoon, and my grandmother would be standing at the front door waiting for us. She wore a flowing, long-sleeved dress and a light kerchief covering her hair, now pure white. My grandmother was a little creature of flesh and bones. Even as a child, I could encircle her with my arms without touching her body. She gripped me with rough hands, pocked and ruined by time, and kissed my head, brow, cheeks, shoulders and hands. No one kissed me as passionately as my grandmother did. She kissed with a unity of body and soul; there was no hiding how she felt. She kissed and kissed and could not stop; she would keep kissing until I slipped from her hands and dashed next door to my aunt's shop.

My aunt was always standing at the shop's front door, also waiting for us to arrive. I hugged her, and she always kissed me with the measured passion of a physicist, no more and no less. My aunt wore an embroidered dress too, and a light kerchief that revealed a few strands of hair, dyed a lustreless black with hints of red that flashed in the sunlight. She had a plump figure, large breasts, and an absent-minded smile that hung on her lips even in moments of sadness. My aunt lived in perpetual sadness. She complained constantly about life and her place in it, and never stopped bemoaning the 'rotten luck' that had been following her since the day she was born. My aunt attributed every tragedy to her luck. 'Some people are just lucky' was her motto in life, a phrase she would slip between sentences as if to grease the words.

My grandfather usually entered the house from a door connected to her shop. I often saw him sitting in a big chair holding the Quran, repeating verses which, though he had memorised them by heart, he still read from the pages throughout the day. He always smiled cheerfully at me, and I do not know what I found so irksome about our relationship. I would kiss his large, drooping cheeks, and he would ask, 'How are you, Grandpa?', calling me by his own name to show how dear I was to him. 'How's Mama? What's new? What brings you here this time? Don't you love us any more? D'you like the Sham better?' This was my grandfather, constantly admonishing me in jest, and never pausing for me to answer. He did not want to hear what I might say; all he wanted was to chastise. My grandmother always shushed him, murmuring in her soft, delicate voice. Had I inherited her animosity? I did not love him the way I should have done. My grandmother did not love him. She complained about how stingy and controlling he was. But she never reproached him: she did not know how. All she knew was how to love. Scolding was the speciality of my grandfather and aunt. They did not chide me because they actually missed me or resented me. Their chastisement was born of a complex relationship between the countryside, where they lived, and the capital, Damascus, where we did; between my father and his Sunni Damascene wife, the woman who had stolen him and stolen me too! I was constantly reprimanded for a sin I had not committed: 'coming from nothing', ignoring my roots, acting like I was better than them. I could never defend myself because this sin was undeniable, a given. Any interaction we had began from this premise.

My grandmother often sat next to me on their long sofa, holding my little hand in hers, kissing me and ruffling my hair and generally showering me with affection. She always brought me to the kitchen so I could keep her company while she made coffee for my father and grandfather in the big coffeepot. The kitchen table was low, as if made just for me. The wicker chairs were low, too. All the houses in the village had chairs like these. I don't know why. Maybe they made sitting more intimate, less formal. In the kitchen, my grandmother asked me questions while she made coffee. 'How are you all doing? How is your mother, and school, and your father's health?' My grandmother was silent after each question. She always waited for my response.

Her habit was to go to sleep at nine and wake at four thirty, but she never went to bed before my father and I came home at night. Sometimes we stayed out until midnight visiting relatives or friends, and we would always come back to find her slumped on the sofa, her hands in her lap, one palm resting in the other. Her neck bowed, her head listing to the left or right. Our footfall always woke her. 'Why haven't you gone to bed, Ma?' my father would ask. She never admitted she was waiting up for us, so as not to make us feel bad. She always said she had been sitting there and must have nodded off. Then she would wait until I had changed into pyjamas. She tucked me into my metal-framed bed, and unfurled the pink mosquito net. Winter was cold in the village and we only had primitive heaters, which did not work when the power went out. My grandmother always covered me with a thick woollen blanket; I remember the weight on my body and how, lying beneath it, I could hardly move. I slept on my back with my arms by my sides under the blanket until morning. Once, a gecko woke me in the middle of the night; I glimpsed him slip into a crack, and then scurry up and down the wall of my room, whose window looked out onto a little vegetable garden. Sometimes my grandmother told me bedtime stories. She instructed me to sleep on my right side so as not to put pressure on my heart, and I would end up facing the cold wall, my nose pressed against the mosquito net. My grandmother lay down next to me in her long white nightgown and thick kerchief, which always smelled clean. She wore woollen winter socks called *qalsheen*, and I don't remember ever seeing her toes. She told me folk tales each night, which she thought were marvellous, and always concluded with a moral. Never content just to tell the story, she always explained the moral to be sure I understood. 'There once were two men who climbed a mountain, hunting for game to eat. All of a sudden, the mouth of a cave yawned opened before them. They went inside, and what did they find? A pile of gold coins! The first man put as many as he could carry in his bag and left. The second man filled up his bag all the way, and his jacket pockets too, and even put a few coins in his mouth! But they were so heavy that he couldn't move. So he emptied his pockets until they were lighter and he began to leave, but then changed his mind and came back to fill them up again. He went back and forth, and back and forth, until night fell . . . and the mouth of the cave closed up. And he died there, alone.' Then she would pause. 'See, little lady,' she would say. 'See, light of my eyes? *Nothing good can come from greed.*'

One morning I woke up at six. My father was still sleeping in his bed next to mine. I got up, trying my best not to make a sound, but my metal bedframe didn't cooperate; it always grated and creaked with the slightest movement. I crept out of the room, slowly, and I'm almost sure that my chronic stomach cramps – the same ones he suffered – have their origins in that moment. My grandfather sat in the living room reading the Quran. 'Good morning, Grandpa,' I shouted. He had trouble hearing. He nodded and smiled. 'Hello, hello . . .' he replied. I went into the cold little kitchen, where my grandmother gave me a hug and made me breakfast, the best I have ever tasted in my life: scrambled eggs cooked in olive oil, fresh home-made labneh, a little plate of hummus, olives, special cheese she made herself, za'atar and olive oil, and bread, fresh from our neighbour Leila's bakery. Leila made bread to order for people in the village. With some neighbours' encouragement she added more salt; for those with high blood pressure she used less. Either way, it was delicious. Whenever Leila was ill and absent from the bakery for a day or two, talk of bread was on everyone's lips.

The village mosque shared a wall with my grandfather's house. This annoyed my father, and made it harder for him to stand our infrequent visits to the village. I never saw a prayer rug in anyone's home in the village, and we visited many. People fasted, but never prayed. During Ramadan, when they broke their fast at Iftar dinners, some people drank moonshine – 'A sip brings you closer to God,' my grandfather would often say. Shortly after the only mosque in the village was built, the one adjacent to his house, children passing by the door glimpsed the sheikh leading prayer. He stood, then kneeled and touched his forehead to the floor, then went up on his knees. They laughed and made fun of him; how indecent he looked! 'Look-at-him-trying-to-do-a-headstand!' they giggled.

When I sat at my grandparents' low table and reached among all the plates of food, my grandmother, whom I rarely saw eat, was always content just to watch me attentively and tell me stories. She often told stories about my father. How, when she was nine months pregnant, my grandfather awoke one night in a panic, terrified, sweat streaming from his brow. He had dreamed that my grandmother had given birth to a baby boy on land he owned in nearby al-Wata, but that a hawk had swooped down and snatched the child from her arms. My grandmother told me that she had worried about my father from the moment of his birth. How could she not, when he was her only child? Later, she became pregnant with my aunt, but her line of descendants ended there. Oh, the prophecies would be fulfilled one day. A hawk would snatch him from her arms.

My grandfather had been married before, but I never met the other woman, and did not even know if she was still alive. She was the mother of the one uncle I had met only recently, and the other uncle who died from drinking tainted moonshine, and my eldest aunt, the one I knew nothing about except for how she treated my disabled uncle. My grandfather loved me, I was certain of that. But children have a sixth sense for things. They pick up on love, hatred, caution and worry. At times a look of envy would shoot from my grandfather's eyes, probably unintentionally. He didn't acknowledge his children with his first wife, and had broken off contact. I only remember seeing them and their children in the house on rare occasions. My grandfather hoped my mother would eventually give birth to a boy, but she developed a benign tumour in her womb after having me, and could no longer conceive. My grandfather never stopped trying to convince my father to marry again, so that his 'only son' might give him a grandson.

My aunt and her daughters teased me constantly when I was little, calling me 'darkie', because of my brown skin. My cousins had light skin, blue eyes and light hair, and were mad about staying white. They shied away from the sun, and bought little jars of thick, sticky cream called Daboul from a shop near their house, which they daubed on their faces twice a day to make themselves whiter. Not only was the cream laced with mercury, but they applied it with an aluminium wand made for polishing copper utensils. They smeared it on their bodies after showering, and rubbed it in so vigorously that their skin turned red. I usually came to visit during the summer, and spent most of my time on the beach, swimming and playing until the sun's last light was extinguished. Then I would head home on foot. The way back was harder than the way there, because the village was perched on top of a mountain overlooking the sea. After just one week of my two-and-a-half-month summer vacation, I would be noticeably more tanned, and they increased the pitch of their taunts, teasing me both for the colour of my skin and for my skinny frame.

While my grandfather was never bothered by my brown skin, he did complain constantly about my clothing. When August arrived, the temperature climbed past 35, and the air grew unbearably sticky and humid. He would call to me as he always did, 'Oh, Grandpa! Cold, so cold! Forget that skirt, eh, go and put on some trousals ... Better than catching your death of a cold with the next slap of wind. No one wants that, eh?' I never paid attention to what he said and insisted on wearing clothes I was not allowed to wear in Damascus. My father was not the one who forbade revealing clothing; it was my mother who feared me being harassed in the bustling neighbourhood where we lived.

Mostly, my grandfather maintained an outward indifference towards me, as if I were an unexpected visitor simply passing through, translucent and elusive. But I knew that of all his grandchildren, I was dearest to his heart. There were a few reasons for this. First and foremost, I was the daughter of his only son by his second wife – not just any son, but one they rarely saw, the one who had left them at the age of twelve and rarely visited. My grandfather was also known for his tight-fistedness: the amount of time he spent sitting in his garden, or wandering between the grapevines and lemon, orange, fig and pomegranate trees, counting the fruits to see whether a grandchild had stolen a lemon or an orange, was not insignificant. But he always encouraged me to pick and eat them, even though I had never loved citrus. He also hid bunches of bananas on top of the fridge and lifted me up to eat one whenever I wanted. I thought, somewhat amused, that he did so because he knew I had a small appetite and wouldn't eat much. On holidays, he gave my aunt's daughters, all several years older than me, three lira. But me, I got ten. At the time, a bottle of fizzy Kazouza cost five lira. A box of biscuits was two and a half. In other words, what seemed to him an enormous sum was actually worth rather little. My grandfather's understanding of economics was stuck in the feudal era; in his mind, the value of money did not change. He thought us extravagant if we spent fifty or one hundred lira in a single day. He was never ashamed to ask what his children's salaries were, or those of their friends. For him, a man's worth was his net worth. When my youngest cousin married a man from a different sect years later, my grandfather became angry and refused to welcome them into his home. He did not let the matter go, either, until he learned that her husband's monthly salary was ten thousand Syrian lira, which at the time was around two hundred dollars. This was below average, given the slow creep of inflation, but in my grandfather's eyes it was a fortune. He raised his eyebrows in disbelief and yelped, 'O Creation! How's a man to spend a sum like that? What do you *do* with ten thousand?' To him, a salary like that was enough to buy a plot of land and build a house. The figure single-handedly conquered his sectarianism, and any concerns that a future grandchild might squander the family's wealth and property. (That 'property' amounted to nothing more than his house and a small plot of land in al-Wata worth less than an old jalopy.) Not only did my cousin's husband make ten thousand lira a month – a fantastical sum as far as my grandfather was concerned – he also renounced Sunnism and converted to Alawism! Sheikhs from our village and surrounding ones paid him visits, he learned the Alawite tenets, and soon began boasting about his ascent through the social ranks. Eventually he went to the Aleppo records office and officially changed his name from Dibo to Ali. He was vigilant about the change, and snapped at anyone who forgot his new name and called him by the old one.

As I've said, according to my aunt, bad luck was to blame for all her misfortune. It was also to blame for the fact that her three daughters were still unmarried and living at home, having failed in all their relationships with men. At that time, the eldest was thirty-five, the middle one was thirty and the youngest one was twenty-six. Three girls who, apart from the eldest, had not finished their education, who lounged around all day and only helped with housework when their mother unleashed a storm of shouting that burst through the house, filled our street and engulfed the whole neighbourhood. I remember my youngest cousin (the one who eventually married Dibo, who would become a 'mighty Alawite-y') for her thunderous voice, which also echoed through the side streets when she was angry. And I remember how careful my aunt always was to contain her daughter's voice, for fear of causing a scandal. 'Oh, won't you shut up, shut up! D'you want to disgrace us in front of the entire neighbourhood?' It was a phrase I soon knew by heart, even though I did not understand what my aunt meant by 'disgrace'. It seemed she was always trying to keep some scandal or another from reaching the ears of 'our chatty neighbours', as she called them. But the phrase was not enough to contain my youngest cousin, or the voice that burst from her chest and boiled up through her white skin, turning it beet-red. No power on earth could contain her voice.

My aunt's husband was never quite able to steer life the way he wanted. He taught Arabic at a primary school and largely enjoyed respect – from everyone except his wife and daughters. He died young, so I never knew him well. My memories of him feel distant, sheathed in a layer of dust. I remember the smile that never left his lips, as if it were a permanent feature. I remember something he often said when he came across me in the house or on the street, a phrase always accompanied by a sigh and a shake of his head: 'Ya, ya, ya . . . What can we do? God knows, God knows.' I had no idea what he was talking about.

I remember him with a book in his hand, reading and shaking his head. He was the only one who read in that great listless house, where the walls were bleak beige and a suppurating smell emanated from the furniture. The sofas arranged in the living and dining rooms gave off the scent of decay, of layers of skin accumulating and gradually disintegrating, day after day, and then being absorbed by the fabric. My aunt's husband never sat on the sofas, as if he had seen the skin cells sloughing off his children, relatives and visitors every day. Instead, he always dragged a wicker chair from his room and positioned it along-side. He sat there reading peacefully, occasionally nodding and smiling. Medium height, with sagging skin around his forearms and neck. A small paunch rounded out his slender frame. He was soft-spoken and moved through the house slowly, within care-fully charted bounds, as if those circumscribed paths were the only way he belonged to this place, the only one he had. As if he were a transient, unwel-come visitor. I never understood why the family found his presence so burdensome, when he was as light as an apparition, barely rippling across the surface of their lives. It vexed them, how different he was. Not only were there differences of opinion, but also a deep, fundamental distinction that permeated their outlooks on life, their moral compasses. His presence was a constant reminder of their own failures and deficiencies, of the void where they frolicked flip-pantly, unconcerned with where destiny was leading them. It made them uneasy, the way he never surren-dered to misfortune.

When their youngest son failed his graduation exams for three years in a row, my uncle said it was because the boy was lazy and uninterested in school-work. Luck had nothing to do with it. But my aunt insisted that bad fortune had played a part, and that his fellow students 'did him in', though who knew why. That's how she was, my aunt. Year in and year out, her sense of injustice swelled in her soul, and her grievances blossomed into one failure after another. I don't know why she felt that way. She never spoke candidly about it, she would just shake her head and press her lips in a forced, aggrieved smile. Then she would sigh, open her small eyes wide, and usually end up in tears.

She was my grandmother's only daughter, and had been married off to a cousin whom I was never sure she loved. Her father gave her a house next door to his with two rooms facing the street, so she could turn one into a shop and the other into the storeroom. Through all of this, my aunt never abandoned her sense of having been wronged. Maybe she dreamed of a better marriage. Her kind cousin was not the right fit for her; she wished he was more of a hustler, quick to grab things by the horns and exploit the corrupt system in which they lived, to improve their lot in life. She complained constantly, was never content or satisfied. Her shop was among the first in the little village, and children from streets near and far came to buy things, especially on weekends and holidays. Women in the village found it a burden to travel to Tartus to do their shopping and began coming to her even if they were not on speaking terms. But I saw how she overcharged customers, even as her long-suffering tears flowed. The shop barely brought in enough to make ends meet, she complained, but

I knew it was always crowded. I remember the store-room we passed through to exit my grandfather's house, and how she filled it with boxes of Kazouza, beer and moonshine, and bags of snacks and dry goods. When her husband passed away, my aunt stopped crying. She became more fickle. They all became more fickle.

Back in Damascus, my father spent four days in the hospital each month, lying in a narrow bed, under an ocean of nausea from the weeks of chemo-therapy. My mother spent nights on the wards with him, and since I was only ten at the time, my aunt came all the way from Tartus to stay with me. They were incredibly lonely times. Right from my return to school, my aunt talked non-stop about the hardships she faced. I remember how exhausting it was to have her around. The way her presence filled a room, then overflowed, leaving no space in the house for any-one else. She slept in my bed, next to me. I could never fall asleep. I would feel my body sliding towards the middle where she lay sleeping, her body carving a canyon into the mattress. I would press my body against the rough, cold wall, as tight as I could, all while she snored and snored. Then in the morning she would say, 'I didn't shut my eyes all night . . . I don't know why I couldn't sleep . . . Maybe it's the pillow . . . Oh, not a wink.' My aunt snored all night but had not managed to sleep! Neither did she eat.

Nor defecate. An angel in human form! That was the self-image she sought. Despite her hefty build and ample belly, she would say that her stomach was so empty, she felt dizzy. In the evenings we sat in the living room, watching a series on one of the few Syrian TV channels there were at that time. Her head slowly drooped and she would slip into a deep slumber. I always nudged her awake so that she could go to bed and she would say, 'I wasn't sleeping ... I wasn't sleeping ... I just closed my eyes to rest ... Why don't you watch the show?' At the time, I had no idea what it meant for a woman brushing fifty to leave her home in the village and come to Damascus every month to stay with her brother's only daughter.

* * *

I have not spoken to Kamil for an entire year. It has been four and a half years since I moved to Beirut. I am afraid of calling and being unable to reach him. I just swallowed half a Xanax as I write this. The urge to cry moves through my chest. But not just the urge to cry. Something deeper. The urge to rip up my memories by the roots – all of them. My memories pain me; they cannot be placated. They bubble up and gallop around so suddenly, colliding with each other and boiling over, and I become a tortured soul confined within my body. Has Kamil left Damascus? Has he closed the door to his office and left like everyone else? How could he abandon us? Who will keep me on track? And the thick white pages he wrote on, where he disentangled and scattered me, are they still in his white metal filing cabinet? Or has he burned them? The cabinet looks like a morgue refrigerator. In its drawers rest dozens, perhaps hundreds, of souls. Records of their lives written in shorthand. I can see Kamil gently opening the drawer and searching nonchalantly for my page. I am terrified that my life can be reduced to a page. A single page for six years? That's how long I had been seeing Kamil. He never needed another one, and there was still room to write more. I told him my memories were haunting me, I told him about the tumult in my head, I told him how afraid I was of falling to pieces. And every time, he gave that cryptic smile, one that even after all those visits I still cannot decipher. An even smile, which blended subtle mockery of my fears (his way of trying to ease my terror and calm me down) with a studied dose of compassion so faint I could barely sense it before it vanished. Then his smile would vanish too, as suddenly as always, behind the thick smoke that seeped from his nostrils and lips. He would give an understanding nod, as if holding my hand to help me cross to a different topic or memory. As if opening the door to my soul and vanquishing the fears he found there. Then he would nod again, to a different tempo this time, something between evasion and conclusion. Only Kamil could end the session. I was not allowed to end it when I felt like it. My feelings were second to his, which came to mirror my soul. It was complicated. I still am not brave enough to contact him.

Every appointment, I climbed the stairs all the way to the third floor. My exhaustion and anxiety quickly made it hard for me to breathe, and I always stopped in front of the wooden door to catch my breath. Then I would enter the waiting room and sit in my usual chair, if it was free. Leila always welcomed me with a warm smile. Leila-cat, I called her, just like her father did before he passed. Often I arrived early so I could sit with her a little while. We smoked and chatted about life, speaking in French if the waiting room was filled with patients. For me, time with Leila-cat was like an extension of my appointment. Or perhaps she tended to my conscious side, while Kamil dealt with the unconscious. I talked to her about life, and she shared her experiences, too. If I left my appointment crying or falling apart, Leila-cat let me into the little kitchen, whose door was otherwise closed, and made me coffee while I calmed down. Once she brought red wine that a relative had fermented. We tried it in the kitchen, unbeknownst to everyone in the waiting room. I usually felt exhausted at the end of my fifty-minute session, my head jostling with questions and confusion. As if Kamil had led me to the only way out, and then abandoned me there. I could see the path clearly and knew it was my only route, but I felt paralysed, unable to take a step forward. I hesitated. As if waiting would fix things. But things are still in limbo. And while desperately trying to resolve my indecision, I have discovered a kind of happiness. How can I live without dreams? I wish I were more decisive. Is there anything worse than realising your dreams? After that, what is left? Isn't it demoralising to finally catch hold of a dream, just to realise you have to go chasing another one?

I had dreamed of living in Beirut for so long, but when it finally happened, quickly and unexpectedly, I do not ever remember feeling so lonely, not since I was a child. There, at the heart of that loneliness, was a nagging question about where I belonged. Had I not got past my desire to belong? Hadn't I gone decades believing that I did not belong among the people with whom I lived, or the houses in which I lived? When did this dark loneliness materialise? Was it when I came to Beirut?

August, four and a half years ago, meant sticky heat, and annoyance at the prospect of moving somewhere new. The sense of isolation I experienced at home in Damascus was accompanied by a deep, desperate desire for any kind of reassurance, and I had begun to conjure such comfort in the smallest of places. I felt a sense of belonging in my bed; there I could take refuge. I identified with my black notebook, with photographs I looked through when I felt I couldn't breathe. With the kitchen window that looked out on our neighbour's garden, and all the trees and activity there. Even my cup of coffee gave me the sense that I belonged. So did favourite chairs in homes I stayed in or visited, chairs which became the only place I could relax. Waking up at six was how I rooted myself in time; if I ever slept in, the day disintegrated around me. For years I only felt I belonged when among certain friends. How could I bring all this with me to Beirut?

When I travelled back to Damascus to see Kamil, he told me I was intentionally sinking into a depression. He noted that I had refused to find myself a real house, and instead chose to live in an apartment that looked more like a bland hotel room. Not only was I avoiding adjusting to Beirut or cultivating a sense of belonging, but I was insisting on keeping my new home temporary. That temporariness has lasted four and a half years. They have passed in a blink, but are still painful and fraught. What kept me from seeking stability? asked Kamil. He reminded me that renting a house did not mean I wouldn't return to Damascus. That was a delusion, a pessimistic one. I was capable of choosing stability, even if just for a week, Kamil said. But I rejected any semblance of belonging or stability.

Everything I did was temporary. Work was temporary, friendships too. So were my apartment and its furnishings. The tiny kitchen occupied part of the tiny living room, and for the first year and a half the only things I kept in the cupboard were three plates, three spoons, three forks and three knives. Plus a coffee mug, and a cup for tea. Only ever enough food for a day, as if I might return to Damascus at any moment. Just a few clothes, as if I had packed for a two-day trip. I had not put my suitcase back in the closet after returning from my latest trip to Damascus. It stayed in the bedroom, open, to make me feel I could return whenever I wanted. I often went to bed early, just to be done with the day. Was there more? I told myself that my new friends, who eased my weary loneliness as best they could, were no more than passing acquaintances. Subconsciously, I maintained our initial reserve. We might spend hours together, but they could sense the sharp contours of the distance between us. This distance became another thing to which I could belong. Beirut became familiar, but my longing for Damascus still burned. Damascus, where I would not return for a long time.

Kamil told me not to keep a journal, but he never told me not to borrow from other people. I ran away from my journal and into others' lives. I did not tell them I wanted to escape from my own memories by stealing theirs. For years I lived in a fugue state, and

I yearned to flee from everywhere to anywhere. Running away was the only way I knew how to leave, and I did not know where I was going! I walked and ran and sweated and my beating heart nearly tore through my chest, but I could not see my footsteps or the asphalt of the road where my feet fell. I could only see my thoughts and memories, urging me to run.

All I remember about the living-room shutters is the chirping sound they made. This was the first comfort I found, the first time I was tempted to escape. Each day between four and five in the afternoon, as the sky turned a gauzy red, the slender space between two buildings – what I could see from the kitchen balcony door – became my refuge. I dreamed that another world awaited me behind these Soviet-style buildings: side-by-side cement blocks, dismal and grey. Their small windows and narrow balcony doors let in little light and always made them seem extra cramped.

I watched the neighbours, still strangers to me, spend all day at home, moving from the living room to the balcony to the kitchen. No social lives to speak of, no visitors or commotion to signal a boisterous life. That was what troubled me, as I observed them from behind a thin pane of glass. Their lives unfolded behind the thick drapes, and at night when their lights were on I spied through the cracks between curtains, where their movements were clear. I loved spying on the neighbours, learning their habits and moods and inventing stories. Windows enthralled me.

As a child, whenever I rode in a taxi with my mother or father, I passed time by staring into buildings, catching a glimpse of the colour of their walls, or the shapes of people's lamps – from dull, depressing neon to sparkling chandeliers. In the worlds of these houses viewed from afar, fantasy, reality, mood, taste and dreams all merged. I often daydreamed about moving into a normal house with a view of a beautiful house, not the other way around. Walls had always incited my desire to flee, windows too, especially those of the school I attended from ages four to eighteen. The classrooms on the second and third floors had large windows set with a gridwork of bars out of fear of the students escaping! School always felt like a prison, and if we had not been released at half-past one in the afternoon every day, it truly would have been one. I remember spending ages sitting by the window with its thick bars, watching the lively narrow street below. I envied the people passing by, imagining them on their way to work or a nearby café.

After I graduated, I felt a flash of joy whenever I passed my old school. I walked by like a woman liberated, unconcerned with what took place behind those rusty iron bars. I enjoyed standing beneath the window of the classroom where I had spent all of secondary school, watching students cross behind the window and wave to passersby as if in a psychiatric ward, blowing kisses here and there and giggling nervously at boys walking past. Then I would hear the teacher shout, angry as all teachers always were. She would yell at the students to return to their seats and keep quiet, and I would be struck by a mad desire to shout joyfully that I was standing in the street, freed from the yoke of authority I had lived under for fifteen years.

Liberating ourselves from the climate of hatred, terror and uncertainty of our long school years was no easy feat. The headmistress hated the teachers, the teachers hated each other *and* the students, and the students hated each other in turn. Each classroom had a student monitor, distinguished by a green band she wore on her right upper arm. She hated us and we hated her back. It was the monitor's duty to ensure that the class ran smoothly, and to take revenge on certain classmates for old disputes by inventing arbitrary accusations. She was responsible for keeping a notebook of allegations, observations and complaints, and recorded evaluations of her fellow students' behaviour, like whether or not they were quiet for all of their six classes every five-and-a-half-hour school day. Every time the class monitor filled a notebook, her title and position were further secured.

Being class monitor was not just an exercise in the

activities of an informant – writing careful 'reports' on one's peers, sowing doubt about the identity of one's sources, and selling their secrets to the highest bidder – the monitor also enjoyed incredible privileges. She gained the admiration of teachers, headmasters, instructors, custodians and other staff, and she never needed to ask her mother to make her a sandwich because she could be confident that other girls would always offer her theirs. The monitor could sit at the front of the class for as long as she wanted, and everyone was careful not to do anything that might anger her. Most students were eager to play the role of monitor, though a few never seemed interested. As for me, I would have loved to be monitor! Though I don't know from where my desire to lord over others arose. How did a girl who grew up in a house free of authority become eager for power?

Aside from the class monitor, there was also a gang of girls who terrorised other students, especially the younger ones. In particular, the Speaker of the People's Council had a daughter who was always surrounded by a ring of ruthless girls. She swaggered through the schoolyard with arms poised and ready, and undid her blonde ponytail, even though loose hair was forbidden at school. She also kept her school uniform jacket tied around her waist, another sin according to our military-education instructor.

She and her little mafia roamed the schoolyard engaging in their favourite game: selecting a student at random and slapping her, pulling her hair or kicking her. She never stopped until the girl screamed louder and louder and pleaded for mercy, while the rest of her little clique laughed.

One time I was her chosen prey. I was skipping rope with a friend when she came up behind me, yanked my long ponytail and slapped me across the face. It was the first slap I had received in my life, and the last. I remember the deep red marks her fingers gouged in my cheek, and how they lasted for hours. I felt insulted, and cried feverishly.

Yes, the schoolyard was where students experimented with ways of life they might later lead in Assad's Syria. A place to train, to learn to cast silent insults and be drilled on obeying the powerful and respecting the authoritative. Students learned to ridicule each other, and find weakness in girls from families of moderate means. They learned to make fun of girls whose fathers did not buy them new coats or trendy, expensive shoes. Our uniforms, which were invented 'to create equality between students and erase class differences,' were a joke. These differences were on clear display in the wool sweaters worn under our uniforms during bitter Levantine winters. Black leather shoes, too, marked the difference between the rich, middle class and poor. Some girls bought new school bags every autumn, while others carried the same one for years until the colour faded, the fabric grew thin and the design had worn away. Pens, notebooks, erasers and pencil sharpeners: any of these school supplies could arouse jealousy or defeat in the hearts of penniless students. The daily allowance given to children by their families every morning was another indication of poverty or wealth. Some students arrived at school with just two lira, others with five, and others with one hundred or one hundred and fifty.

When Naseem hung up on our call, receding into himself, all I could hear was silence. It was comforting somehow, as if I'd suddenly closed my eyes. Closure, here, wasn't just a physical act; I felt as if I'd closed my eyes, heart and soul. All my fears and anxieties were instantly extinguished and replaced by a sense of levity. As if everything that came before, and everything that was still to come, could be taken lightly. As if I could take my memories lightly. I've dreamed so often of letting my mind be dispersed by the wind, allowing my memories to drift away, of finally being able to relax. I've wished so hard to forget who I am, what I want, where I was born, whom I've lived with, who my friends were, where I've walked, which streets I, or my loved ones, have lived on. I want to forget, to lose my memory completely, all at once. Because I know that memory is either there or it's not. You either come to terms with memories – their heavy-handedness or fragility, their terror or joy – or you rid yourself of them for good, so completely that you forget your own name. *I* wanted to forget my own name. Forget my name? Really? Or did I want others to forget it? Was *I* the source of my suffering, or was this just what others expected of me? (For years I'd been convinced that I hated myself. Then one day I woke up and discovered that I loved myself, that I am deserving. Other people were what troubled me; the people I put up with, those I put on my shoulders and carried for years until a certain distaste dragged me down. I thought it was an aversion to myself. Eventually I realised that I missed myself, missed the person I am. I longed to be light and alone, to live on my own terms.) Why do we exhaust ourselves doing what others want, fulfilling their wishes, and reassuring them? What is the point in reassuring others while we live in anxiety and fear?

That morning, I got out of bed feeling terribly hungry, as if I hadn't eaten a bite since the day before. (To be honest, I don't usually eat much. I've developed an aversion to food. Food is my adversary. I pick up a piece of bread as if it's a rock I have to swallow, which might lodge itself in my throat, make its way down to my stomach and fill me with lethargy. I don't dare to eat much any more. As soon as food touches my stomach I feel weary and fatigued, as if I've eaten a whole sheep. Hunger makes me feel safe: an empty stomach signals an empty mind, memory and soul. I love that empty feeling. I frolic in it, like a single small cloud in a vast, savage sky. Hunger makes me feel light, it frees me from all my tiresome obligations, even the duty of digestion. The digestive process requires more effort than I can handle now. My heart has to beat faster than usual, my intestines contract and release, and my stomach emits gurgling sounds.)

As I got up, I found myself enjoying the sensation of hunger, knowing that despite how famished I was, I would eat very little. I left my bedroom and went into the living room. My mother was sitting on the red sofa, holding a book she'd started weeks ago. I swear she'd been staring at the same page, page 24, for days. (My mother has become a lean little thing, heaped on the sofa under a thin blanket, constantly reading a sentence, repeating it out loud to herself and then reading it again. As soon as she moves on to the next sentence, she discovers that she needs to reread the previous one, the sentence she's read again and again. She stares at the sentence, reads it, and then reads it again. I don't know if she's really reading all the time, or if she's just chosen to stare at a book instead of at empty space. Space makes her feel crazier. She hasn't lost her mind, but she thinks she has.) Recently, my mother told me she was going to develop Alzheimer's soon. I teased her and told her to hurry up. She shot me a look, and then gave a strange smile. I didn't completely understand, but I caught a certain bitterness beneath her secretive, fleeting grin. My mother had always had a charming smile. She, who was so good at laughing and being happy, was now reduced to a poor little creature under a thin blanket. I told her that Alzheimer's eases the burden of dying.

'It lets us look forward to death instead of fearing it,' I told her. 'It gives us reason for celebration instead of grief.'

'*Us*? Who's "*us*"?' she asked me.

I said nothing.

My mother had been sitting on the sofa reading page 24 for days. Suddenly she had aged. I couldn't comprehend it. When we'd gone to bed she had been a young woman, and when we woke up she was old. I told myself I was lucky she had aged overnight and not at midday; that would have been terrifying. (If she had gone into the kitchen to make breakfast, for instance, and come out a few minutes later, having grown old. Or if she'd said, in her exasperatingly soft voice, 'Suleima, I'm going to take a shower,' and then emerged from the bathroom an old woman.) It really was lucky that my mother had aged overnight, and we'd only woken up to find she was old.

Who's 'us'? Just her and me now. My brother, Fouad, disappeared two and a half years ago. When that happened my mother didn't age: she cried a lot, but she didn't grow older.

Was it the tears? Maybe. Tears cleanse the soul, as my mother says. Or maybe she cried instead of ageing, maybe she could only do one of the two. She cried a lot, so feverishly that her tears dried up. (This often happens to

69

me, too.) And then, when the last of her tears were gone, my mother fell asleep a young woman and awoke an elderly one. I didn't tell her that I hadn't slept since Fouad disappeared. I didn't tell her that every night, every day and every moment, I was wishing for him to die. I prayed, pleaded with God and memorised verses of the Quran, so the Lord would hear my prayers and respond. I tried in vain to push my brother's image from my mind.

In the first few months after his disappearance, I thought that I'd see him in my imagination if I shut my eyes, so I didn't. Night after night I kept myself from closing my eyes, until I was so exhausted that I became weak and finally slept for a few hours. I woke up somewhat re-energized, and then kept my eyes open again, night and day, for weeks . . . and on, and on. I said nothing to my mother about this, and she said nothing to me. I felt certain she wished he would die, too. How could a mother's heart rest if her son were alive, being tortured endlessly? To ease my mind, I told myself that a mother's heart knows, that she could sense whether Fouad was gone from this world, that's how she could sleep in peace. She must know . . . how else could she have kept going all those months? But now she'd aged overnight, even if she was calmly sitting on the sofa and reading page 24.

I once told Kamil that when I was little, I imagined by father and brother being abused, beaten and tortured. I imagined them drowning. Not in nature, the way Naseem feared; I imagined bad guys drowning and torturing them with delight. Alone in my bed at night, I cried, even though I knew they were nearby in their beds. Kamil and I examined the source of these thoughts and ideas. How was it that a girl of nine or ten, living in a quiet home, not lacking for love or security, had such violent thoughts in her mind! I don't remember how Kamil responded, not exactly. But I do remember him describing this as self-flagellation. Yes, I was self-flagellating, and still am. I saw my father on his knees, kissing someone's feet. Today, I think that person must have been an officer. But I'm not sure if I imagined him as an officer when I was a child, or if the idea of an officer took hold over time, after seeing so many real images like that. Images that are no longer imaginary! There are people forced to kiss officers' feet every second, every day, in this country! Is it that simple? Could you believe it? Don't we discuss in our sessions the fact that someone in the world is dying every minute? Don't we say that every second a mother somewhere is losing her child? We've also started to say that there's a Syrian on his knees every minute of each day, being forced to kiss an officer's feet.

When Fouad disappeared, I blamed myself. What good had my obsessive childhood self-flagellation done? Should I do it again now, for real reasons, not imaginary ones? If I'd known, though, if I'd really expected it to happen, I wouldn't have let myself drown in those thoughts before it was time. I would have enjoyed many peaceful nights' sleep, untroubled by a sick imagination.

I also consoled myself over my father's death. He passed away ten years ago. He didn't die under torture, wasn't beaten like I often imagined. My mother says it was fear that killed him. I don't believe her. Maybe I'd just rather not. My father died. He was seventy. He went to bed and didn't wake up. Not unlike my mother, who went to bed and woke up an old woman. He tried to leap between two worlds, failed, and tumbled down into death. Maybe he preferred dying to growing old. In the end, the 'self-flagellation' that I couldn't disentangle from him passed when he did. After his death, I only imagined him dressed elegantly, and standing, never sitting or kneeling.

*

I was five when we left our hometown of Hama for Damascus. It was 1982, the year of the massacre. I don't remember anything from that period except a handful of images. I go back and forth about whether they're my memories, or memories my mother told me. When it comes to my childhood, I can't distinguish any more between what I remember myself and stories I heard or was told. My mother told me that my father wet himself, asked her to pack up their things and told her they were taking the children and leaving for Damascus. My mother was lost for words. The crotch of my father's brown trousers darkened. I think now about how my mother told us this story one morning after he had passed away. Why did she tell us after he'd died? Why did she want us to

72

know? To convince us that fear was what killed him? She also said that he decided to leave their hometown of Hama even though he was a doctor! That's exactly how she said it. When she finished the sentence, I imagined her mouth being sealed with an exclamation point. She raised her eyebrows and shook her head wryly.

To this day I don't know if she misses him. I have a feeling that when he died, she relaxed. She never says that his death made her happy, but I can see it in her eyes, body and soul. Another time she told us that our father was tormented by the exhausting nature of fear. She said she'd lived through thirty-two years of fear with him, and when my mother said the number, she ground her teeth on each consonant, rending the syllables apart, as if to make us feel the impact of each year, its oppressive weight. 'Thirty-two years!' Yes, Father left his hometown, afraid of the indiscriminate killing he'd witnessed in the streets. He took his family and fled to Damascus, where we stayed after the massacre ended, when everyone else who'd survived returned home and to their former lives. Of course they returned home, but did they really return to their former lives? Could life straighten itself out and settle back into its old rhythm, as if nothing had happened? Can someone who has smelled the scent of death go back to the way things were? My father never spoke to us of Hama. Maybe he managed to do something I haven't been able to: erase it from his memory. He managed to hold on to the memories he wanted.

In Damascus we lived in an area called Ain al-Kirish, and my father rented space for his office in the building we lived in. 'How can he treat patients from Damascus when he turned his back on people from his own city?' This question began to echo in my mind because of how often I heard my mother say it. I felt bad for my father. When I imagined him, my mother and Fouad being tortured, it was my father for whom my heart ached most. I'd watch him, more affected than the others by the pain. I saw his face scrunched up in agony. What crushed me more than anything was the pleading, and the weary muttering, that emerged from his battered mouth. 'Kill me already,' I imagined him saying. 'Oh God, make it stop, I can't take it any more.' And I cried. I missed him at night, so I'd slip out of my bed and into their room, and go to the right side of the bed where my father slept. I stood at the head of their bed. Stretched out my little finger and held it to his nose to be sure he was still alive, even after that bloody torture. (When I read a similar passage in Naseem's manuscript, I saw myself. Naseem stole me and wrote me into his novel. But I don't tell him this.) My mother and Fouad, on the other hand, always resisted! Their expressions never elicited my sympathy. Just the opposite; they were stubbornly brave. My father was the only one who, with just a look, could set my soul afire. Luckily, he died before he was ever stopped at a checkpoint, forced to prove his identity or subjected to humiliating questions.

Did Kamil connect my tendency towards self-flagellation with the Hama massacre and our move to Damascus? I don't think so. When I was young I hadn't known exactly what was happening in Hama, and our lives in Damascus had always been stable. I remember the President's portrait hanging in my father's office. And how it made my mother endlessly angry. 'You hang a portrait of the man who murdered your family? Does that make you happy? It wasn't enough to run away, huh? What kind of man kills someone and shows up at the funeral?' She often asked him this, but never felt the need to answer; she never said, '*You're* the kind of man who kills someone and shows up at the funeral.' I imagine that her constant browbeating wounded and confused him. 'Can you blame other Syrians for shutting their doors in our faces?' she'd mutter. She never called their reaction unwarranted. No, their fellow townspeople had fled Hama, leaving their kin to die alone, and my father had been first out the door. They hadn't aided them, or even stopped by their sides, inhaled the scent of their death, or stared at still-bleeding bodies strewn by the roadside. To this my father would gravely respond: 'It's *because* I'm from Hama that I hang his portrait. Because my sin is greater.' He'd say something like that and then leave the house for his office or the coffee shop where he met with friends. To a certain degree, the portrait was a confession that he didn't belong in Damascus. That he'd broken certain bonds, and then uprooted those memories from his mind. He was tolerant and forgiving, and worked to make amends.

All my father ever wanted was to keep himself and his small family alive. What did my mother hope to gain from all those years of tormenting him, of blame, shame and constant reminders of his 'great betrayal'? What did she want, aside from regaining our dignity? Did she wish we'd stayed in Hama and her husband had been killed? And if he'd been murdered like so many others, would the memory of them be imprinted on her mind? Could death clear the ground for a dignified life? Would my mother have preferred life as an honourable widow to the one she led alongside a 'weak' and 'cowardly' husband 'for thirty-two years' – gritting her teeth on each consonant and the spaces in between?

I once teased Naseem, telling him that he should write about my father, but he never responded to humour unless we were already joking. Yes, Naseem was tediously serious. He wasn't even good at banter. Even when telling jokes or riddles he maintained his monotone and his sternly knitted brows. The stitch in the centre that pulled them together was permanent, as if he'd been born with it. The knot between his brows was firmly tied, as if his soul hadn't sprung from his mother's womb, as if it didn't reside in his chest, but here in this Gordian knot.

Naseem hasn't written my father's story. My mother isn't in the manuscript either. It's *me* he's stolen. I haven't told him this. If I did, he'd be sure to deny it. He'd say that his narrator's story doesn't follow mine at all. And then I'd become flustered and lose my words, because no matter how hard I might try, I wouldn't be able to find tangible proof that I am this unnamed narrator. Why hasn't he given her a name? Is it because he wants to write about me, and while he doesn't dare call her Suleima, he also knows that if he chooses a different name it would disrupt his creative process? That's probably why he's left her nameless. But she *is* me! It's true that her family is different, as are her memories, but our souls clearly spin in the same orbit. I don't say anything to him: I don't have strong enough evidence. If I do, he might say that she and I belong to the same generation and have both lived in Damascus, and have general features in common with all Syrians. We both saw Kamil, too. I don't know how to explain that it's not these traits that make us similar, not even our visits to Kamil. There's something deeper than our generation, country or therapist.

The language of the manuscript also makes an impression on me. It just seems like a diary, written in a somewhat impressionistic and improvisatory style. Maybe he couldn't manage to write a novel about the revolution, and dealt with this weakness by composing a fictional diary instead.

Naseem's manuscript

Back when I lived in Damascus, when the sun rose I felt downcast and alone. But if it hid behind thick, supple clouds, I was thrilled. At night when it slipped from the sky, I would often take my computer and go to a coffee shop near our house. Perhaps when the sun dipped past the horizon, it was setting in my soul, illuminating me from within, so I could shine onto the page? At dawn, when I could see that the sky's radiance was there to stay, I would gather my things and return home, dejected.

I abandoned this routine when I arrived in Beirut. I was unable to write any more. I began to feel frustrated at the sight of clouds and fell out of the habit of reading, too – books had once lined our living-room shelves, but in this house there were only a few, which made me feel even more inadequate. I used to spend most of my time reading; now I was fed up with it, and felt books exposed things in me that I was not ready to reveal. My emotions were held hostage by events in Syria. I hated the Beiruti clouds and rain. They made my true home feel further away, and I hated that I couldn't go back whenever I wanted. Even if I had no immediate plans to return, just thinking about the thick snow and blocked roads made Beirut feel like an airless prison. I remember spending hours browsing Google Earth late into the night. I would zoom further and further out until Damascus appeared on the map, too. I liked knowing that it was not all that far away. Damascus could almost be closer than Tyre.

That first winter in Beirut, I did go back every two weeks, despite the accumulating snow. We got stuck in Dahr al-Baydar on more than one occasion. One time in particular the road was completely obscured and snow was everywhere. I remember even the air was white, infused with falling flakes. Slowly, the light grew softer. Darkness fell. No street lamps to illuminate the roadsides, no signs of life. We were suspended in a place without houses, coffee shops or pharmacies. Just piles of snow, thick flakes on the wind, biting cold, a taxi with the headlights turned off so the driver could save what little petrol remained in the tank, and a wait so long I felt I could not breathe. I felt flushed with anxiety so I opened a window. But it was cold, so I shut it again. Feeling agitated, I got out to walk across the snow, between all the cars stuck behind us and in front of us. I was thirsty, but didn't know where I'd put the water I had brought with me and had been sipping while growing more and more nervous. I got back in the cab. And suddenly I panicked. I was afraid of dying in this enclosed space, afraid of being buried under the snow with all the other cars and their passengers, afraid we would die en masse like Syrians were dying en masse back home. Suddenly, like a miracle, the cars began to move. One by one, we made it down to Chtaura and by the time we arrived, the sense of danger had dissipated. My heart began to beat again. I knew I would soon be home.

I saw Kamil every time I visited Damascus. My appointments were on Saturdays, and it reassured me to make the next one for two weeks' time. Leila told me it was not necessary, that all I had to do was call two days before my next visit. But I insisted. Maybe having an appointment made it easier to return to Beirut. I continued making appointments until my last trip to Damascus, though I had not known beforehand that it would be my last. 'Enough,' Kamil said to me. There was no need to see him any more. I asked him if he had finally pieced me together: bit by bit, memory on top of memory, cell after cell. He nodded. Thinking about it now, maybe he only said 'enough' to give me the opportunity to adjust to Beirut. Maybe he knew how dependent I was on our regular appointments and that this was making it harder for me to adjust to my new life. That it disrupted my growing sense of continuity. Why did I think this? Maybe because my need for him was constant, and my mental state was worsening every day. My breath still caught in my chest. I still wrestled with fear and panic attacks. I still counted the number of steps I took, from early morning until night descended. Anxiety still ran rampant through my body, from the moment the sun rose until it was extinguished, announcing the end of another day. What did I have to look forward to? Nothing, not any more. Not to writing in the mornings, reading books or meeting up with friends. Nothing fun. And it was clear that moving back to Damascus was just a fantasy. War toyed with geography, redrawing roads and borders. My home retreated further every day, until it may as well have been as far as Paris, or London, or Germany.

* * *

I don't know how the rift with my relatives began. Honestly. Cannot remember what started it. There was no clear beginning, no precise date or time. As if we had entered a tacit agreement, without exchanging words, opinions or anything at all. It was a one-sided arrangement, though. One day I discovered that a rift had occurred. At the time, I didn't want to sever our relationship. No blood had been shed, and in my heart I still had ample room for our differences. We could listen to each other and maybe, just maybe (I was not completely sure) we could understand each other's points of view, and forgive. We had always been different, that was true. But our differences had never been political. They just teased me for being brown and took pride in their white skin and blue eyes – and if not blue, at least hazel. Their insults went beyond skin colour to constant accusations that I 'came from nothing' and didn't acknowledge my own history or connection to them. No wonder I never felt I belonged.

There were only a few family members to whom I felt connected. My cousin Farid, for example, was closest to my heart. He was my father's sister's eldest son. I was young when he got married, and he took me with him when he went to his wife's family to ask for her hand. I attended their wedding, and was fifteen when Farid's wife became pregnant with the first of their three children. I visited them often, and we would stay up late on the balcony, which had overlooked the sea until other buildings crowded out the view. Farid, his wife and I would sit around, drinking arak and talking about the family and politics. We held similar views, and only disagreed on superficial things. Farid tended to agree with the opposition, though his reasons were different from mine or most others'. He was a boy from the village who read books, studied philosophy and shared what he learned; he was a boy who had dreams . . . and then found himself trapped in a job at the cement factory, day in, day out, his health failing from exposure to carcinogens. He ended up there because it was the only way to support his family. But the salary was not enough, so he was forced to open a shop selling clothes imported from Turkey. Farid sided with the opposition because he had studied philosophy, though it had little connection with his day-to-day, running himself ragged to ensure his family had a good life.

His youngest brother had all the same reasons to share his politics, but he did not. He realised he was powerless and revelled in the fact. He studied fine arts and became an artist. He taught art at a school in Tartus until he was married, and then suddenly an art teacher's salary was not enough. He ended up playing the darbuka in a seaside nightclub, accompanying the dancers. I once asked him to take me with him so I could watch, but he refused. The place was not suitable for 'people like us'. Even though he worked there! It was 'inappropriate', he said. He also bought an unlicensed gun when he started working at the club. (At the time I did not know it would be used for other ends when the revolution began.)

My eldest cousin, the son of my father's half-brother, was an engineer. We were friendly and saw each other every two or three months. He often visited us in Damascus and spent the night, and we always stayed up late chatting. His wife was from Lattakia, and her family were part of the *shabiha*, Assad's militia. He was not on good terms with them. He tried to distance himself but they threatened to kill him, so he left well enough alone. Two years after the revolution began, this cousin told me that he had killed nine people so far, and would not mind making me the tenth.

On my last visit to Damascus, before Kamil broke my shackles and launched me into the world, I brought up a subject we had discussed before: how my life was filled with women. Previously, I had said all the men in my life were disabled, ill or dead . . . and on that last visit, I added 'or murderers'. Something flickered in Kamil's eyes, a movement I barely caught behind the thick smoke. Was this why he set me free, to protect me from what lurked in Damascus? Maybe he was telling me, 'Go to Beirut, and don't ever come back.' Exactly two months later, my eldest girl cousin wrote me a letter. 'I don't hope they kill your mother, oh no,' she wrote. 'I hope they rape you in front of her, and then slaughter you like an animal, so she spends the rest of her days in agony.' That was what she wrote – my own cousin. The only one of her siblings who graduated from university, and with a degree in English, the one who taught English in Tartus. The only one of the siblings who could read, the one who asked me every time I visited to bring her the best books I had read lately: novels, short stories, plays, philosophy, memoirs and prison diaries.

I remember panicking when I read what she wrote. Trembling at the words. Then came a violent realisation, beyond anything I could handle. How had the rift grown so deep? Was it possible for someone to go to sleep as a human being one night and wake up a vicious beast? Or had the beast simply been hiding, lurking in the body of a woman so educated, loving and refined? Had it simply been waiting until it was needed? Who needed it? No one. It sought sympathisers and found kindred beasts: one had been hiding in the heart of an artist, a man who played the darbuka in a nightclub. Another was lurking in a young wife's heart, a woman whose husband had transformed from Dibo to Ali in broad daylight. Another beast dwelled in the heart of an 'aimless' schoolboy who consistently failed his final exams – a boy who joyfully discovered a desire for power during the revolution. Who joined the *shabiha* and informed on villagers who failed to appear when called up for service 'to flag and country'. Who sent his neighbours to their deaths, and who recently enlisted in Air Force Intelligence Directorate: an informant and a killer.

A beast had emerged from my cousin's mouth,

and that one unleashed the rest. She sicced these beasts on me, and on anyone else who was different. As for me, someone who had always thought my body held a single soul, I realised that a tiny beast was germinating inside of me, too. I wished her dead when I read what she wrote. True, I did not hope she would be raped, or slaughtered like an animal, but I wished her dead! And that was enough.

That bit of savagery was enough for me to realise that we could not live alongside one another, not after that. We didn't want to live side by side. How could either of us live next to a murderous beast? Then her imagination extended to my mother's womb. She said my mother's womb was filthy, and hoped that 'the Sunni womb that bore you rots with cancer'. Then she went further and invoked filthy sperm. I saw myself shrinking, turning into a seed in my mother's womb. I began to see how others could revel in torturing and killing people. They didn't see human beings, just filthy sperm to exterminate.

These beasts who flung insults and joined the shabiha to fight on the side of a regime killing people in cold blood, one day they had woken up and discovered my mother was Sunni! All these years she had lived with my father and alongside them, in the village and in our home in Damascus, and in their homes in Damascus too, all these years and they had not realised. The revolution had opened their blue and green eyes, and they stared at her Sunni-ness. She never insulted anyone. She found their calls to kill us reprehensible, and never discovered they were Alawite! Of course, she had always known they were Alawite. But that did not make them animals in her eyes. She did not see the packs of beasts emerging from their mouths and souls. Just beastly people – because that was what they were, not because they belonged to a certain sect.

The revolution is like a divorce; family members start saying things like, 'She was never right for you anyway! She came from nothing, had no morals . . . you're better off without her.' As if my mother became a divorcée, not a widow, when the revolution broke out. 'She came from nothing, she's Sunni!' Thinking about this is enough to bring on a panic attack. Didn't I want to wipe this from my memory? Rid myself of it completely? A terrible thing, memory. I open it an inch, and all of this rushes out; I hear the thunder of my heart beating, and the crack of electricity regulating its pace.

The rift punctured a hole in my memory. We didn't drift apart slowly; it happened suddenly, without warning. How does a human being become a monster? Does it happen instantly, or is it a slow transformation? Had these monsters lain dormant in their souls? Sleeping when they slept and waking when they awoke, eating and dressing and smoking, and all the while being nourished, growing, waiting for just the right moment to emerge? The revolution erupted in an instant. And in that instant, monsters appeared. They filled our city, our homes, our living rooms. They hit and slapped and insulted and killed and destroyed a whole history of human relationships.

I have this memory of Fouad, my brother. My father had been out, performing an operation at his clinic or the Italian Hospital, I don't remember which. My mother was in the kitchen making dinner. Fouad and I were in the living room, pressed close to the wood stove. Mother turned the television towards us so we wouldn't grow bored and bother her. Channel Syria, the only channel there was at the time, was playing the afternoon news. The newscaster announced that the prime minister was launching a cultural institution, and then the news cut to scenes of the opening ceremony. Silent scenes. The prime minister cut a red ribbon and the attendees applauded, all smiling broadly. But there were no sounds of clapping or laughing. All the men looked alike. The same charcoal suits. Same white shirts. Same thick moustaches. Varying degrees of baldness, but the same dyed hair. Suddenly Fouad shut his eyes and started yelling. Our mother came running into the room. 'Why can't we hear them clapping?' he asked in terror. 'Are they applauding in thin air?'

Fouad later told me how he'd felt the first time he joined a protest with his friends in the Midan neighbourhood. 'I yelled and I heard my voice,' he said. 'Everyone was shouting and clapping. Everyone could hear each other. The age of silence is over!' This last sentence wasn't hyperbole. Fouad meant it. The age of silence that had pervaded our schools, homes and streets – the silence on the television screen that had thoroughly terrified him – was over for good.

Our mother knew that her only son was participating in the protests. She was glad. Maybe she saw it as standing up for rights that had been taken from her and our father; maybe she saw Fouad avenging her. But I was surprised that she urged him to rush out and join in. Wasn't she afraid for him? I asked myself. I didn't ask her. When he disappeared I considered asking her, but I never did. Fouad left for work one day and didn't come home. It was that simple. He went out and didn't come back. That was two and a half years ago. Every day since, I have prayed that he's dead. And my mother, who aged so suddenly, her sense of calm reassures me. He must be dead. How could she be so calm if she knew he was alive?

Fouad was working as an instructor at the Higher Institute for Dramatic Arts. (It's painful to say the words 'was working'. They're the past progressive, an incomplete tense. I want a complete tense, like the past perfect.) Mother wanted him to be a doctor. Just like Naseem's mother wanted for her son. My mother's reasons were different, though. She wanted him to make up for what her 'traitor' husband had done. Was she expecting another massacre? A massacre into which she could send her son, so he could save a new generation in Hama?

Fouad didn't make this desire a reality, though. He wanted to study theatre criticism and become a professor. In a country with little arts funding, where the cultural sector was in crisis and corruption reigned, he chose theatre. The institute was his refuge in this lonely city of Damascus. ('Was', again?) He loved the atmosphere, his students and the geographic and sectarian diversity that had somewhat escaped the regime and security services' grip. Maybe the institute was seen as neutral territory; maybe it was protected because it served a greater power. There at the institute, near the radio and television building and al-Assad Library, a different Syria existed and thrived. That's what Fouad always said, trying to convince me to join him in the performing arts instead of the fine arts. But after the revolution began, that elegant white building coughed up its soul and was possessed by another one. Controversies reared their heads and the security services arrived, armed with weapons and vehicles. Regional and sectarian diversity no longer formed the happy picture that Fouad had once painted. Divisions emerged. Several instructors started to avoid teaching theatre in their lectures, explaining that it was where 'terrorists' gathered – terrorists who intended to kidnap and massacre minorities in cold blood. Then Fouad disappeared. Was the institute a meeting spot for terrorists? Did they think *he* was a terrorist? Did he transform, in their eyes, from a simple colleague into an instructor from Hama; was he held to account for Hama's history?

★

Naseem showed no sympathy when Fouad disappeared; he just looked at me as if to say, 'Didn't I tell you?' He hadn't started hitting himself at that point. He could still look me in the eye and stare into the space around my pupils. The eyes are the centre of one's being. That's what he told me, more than once. Naseem is no good with explanations. He may have written novels about other people, but he's no good at talking about himself. Maybe writing sates him, so he needs nothing more from life? He is silent in life, and speaks on the page? Even when sitting with me, a certain restlessness always moves behind his eyes: he has no patience for conversation. He excels only at silence. And recently, he's begun to excel at self-flagellation.

I know that Naseem isn't processing these events any more. But I still can't understand. He behaves as if he fell into a daze in mid-2011 and just now woke up to discover that his parents' house in Homs was destroyed in the shelling, his mother and only sister died under the rubble and his father is partially paralysed, driven nearly mad by guilt at being the only survivor. Aren't five years enough? Time didn't stop on that day of his great loss. And if Naseem has woken up to find himself alone with a bed-bound father who talks to himself all day, does this mean that Naseem has lost his mind too?

I don't think so. He sent me his manuscript a few days ago. Or was it weeks, months ago? I can't remember any more. Time has lost its meaning. And I still haven't told him that he stole me. He must have sent me the book in an attempt to justify his theft, but I want to tell him to stop writing. To say to him, your imagination is ruined, you clearly can't create characters unless you fill them out with people you know. You've lost your imagination so you're using me: my fears and anxieties, my looks and childhood memories. You stole the parts of myself that I miss, the ones I've been losing for years and never managed to find, because when you lose something, it's gone for ever. There's no way to recover it, and searching is a sure path to frustration and despair.

Why have you written about me, Naseem? Is it because you can't write fiction now? Did you borrow my life to escape your own?

The last time we met, Naseem told me he couldn't write any more. Every time he started a new novel, he'd flounder about in his own experiences and those of his family, and end up sinking deeper into himself. Then he'd toss aside what he'd written and start anew. He said you know you've failed when you start writing about yourself. He said writing is a chance to live among people you don't know.

But he doesn't know *me*!

Naseem's manuscript

I was sitting in the living room, sipping a cup of coffee and smoking my fourth cigarette of the morning. It was around quarter past ten. Um Malek sat to my left drinking her coffee, like she always did when she arrived at the house. Late twenties. Sturdy build. She'd given birth to three children; the eldest was nine and the youngest was three.

A certain melancholy burned beneath her friendly gaze. A profound yet passing sadness, there in the light in her eyes, as if she had happened across the feeling but forbade it from creeping into her soul, where it might take root. She had watchful eyes. And when she spoke, the sadness spilled from her lips until a smile broke through, like the sun cresting layers of snow fallen overnight. She told me what had happened like someone commenting on the weather, letting her words fall matter-of-factly, unaware, perhaps, of the impact she left on her listener. Placid, calm – that was Um Malek. She described things as if they were happening to someone else. As if she were outside the story she told, watching it from afar and protecting herself from succumbing to fear. Fear had no place in her life: fear was a luxury, a disruption that drained the energy she needed to live.

Um Malek was from Homs and knew nothing in Beirut aside from the houses she cooked and cleaned for each day. She knew the tiny room where she lived with her three children in the Burj al-Barajneh refugee camp. Every morning when she went out she left them there, alone. But she did not worry, because worry was a type of fear, and fear was something she could not afford. At night when she returned, she took refuge in their company as they did in hers. 'During the day I'm their child, and at night they are mine.' That was what Um Malek said, as plainly as someone noting a flock of clouds she's seen sweep across the sky. Her eldest son, Malek, was not a child any more. He had sprouted a moustache, Um Malek said, half jesting, barely managing a smile. He was six years old when it appeared. It was the day he stood at the edge of a pit in the ground, looked down and saw his father lying there. He sprouted a moustache and told his mother he wanted to study ophthalmology so he could heal his father's eyes. They were covered with dirt. His father had gone out to protest and a member of the *shabiha* had beaten him to death with a metal truncheon. Not a drop of blood spilled; he had died of internal bleeding.

Every morning when she leaves for work, her son gently tells her, 'Come back tonight . . . don't leave us.'

'Oh, my heart . . .' Um Malek said to me, maintaining a smile the whole time. 'They're afraid I'll leave them like their father did. They're afraid I won't return.'

To change the subject, I asked Um Malek which neighbourhood they had lived in, and she told me, 'Bab Dreib.' She said that her eldest uncle still lives in Homs, but he left the neighbourhood of Bab Dreib when it was destroyed. He goes back once a month to collect his pension and passes by their old house and tells them what he sees. Their home, like most in the area, was taken over by *shabiha* and the regime's army. She said they stole all the furniture. Even ripped lamps off the walls. They used a steam iron to remove the bathroom tiles. Then they ripped up the paving stones. They took the glass from the doors and the double-glazed windows, too. Then they began tearing balustrades off the balcony. Um Malek had heard that one of the warlords who was particularly close to the regime had opened a metal factory.

Hearing Um Malek's words, I walked, in my mind's eye, in the footsteps of the *shabiha*. I followed them from the living room to the bedrooms. Watched them bring an iron into the next room and heat it up

97

to help remove the tiles. With them I ran to the balcony, empty of the family that once sat there, and, now out of breath, ripped out the balustrades. I tried to catch my breath and calm my heartbeat, and I inhaled deeply to ease the tightness in my chest. Um Malek continued talking and I got up and ran to my room.

I looked in the mirror, swallowed a Xanax and let myself cry. How could anyone be so fragile? How could words alone bruise one's soul like a violent blow? How could they conjure a complete memory, instantly restore a whole history? A single word could take my body from where it was seated safely on the sofa and toss it down a well of memory. Left there, a frightened creature, my body fights for life tooth and nail, trying in vain to scramble up and escape. And all it takes to lift it to safety is a single Xanax. Nothing more. I struggle with this contradiction.

I always believed that adversity makes us stronger, more resilient. Should we not be used to death by now? Five years on, did I still need to live in fear? But my fears have not faded; new ones simply accumulate. My brain churns out all types of anxiety, fear, loneliness and terror, while my heart races and my breath grows ragged. Everything toys with my fleeting sense of security, especially at night, when the day draws to a close. I am afraid, so I think about fear. And when I think about fear, I feel afraid. Maybe fear is the only emotion with which the soul wrestles constantly. It is so difficult to resolve, or to coexist with. It nests deep inside, no relation to the outside world. It is dazzlingly innovative and multifarious, reinventing itself at every turn. My imagination blazes in service of fear and anxiety, and baulks at comfort. Perhaps fear is the only way it knows to defend itself.

Is there anything more vivid than fear? Naseem has stolen stories of my father and my fear-flecked childhood, and animated them with his own character. If I tell him this, he will say that my family and I are just four people among twenty-three million frightened Syrians. Or he will tell me flatly that he's also afraid, and has disguised himself too behind a pen name. He will say that he lost his family just like Um Malek lost her husband. That we all have the same story. We may as well be copies of each other. Here we are, at school, at home, in the streets, in Damascus's few cinemas, at the theatre, in government offices . . . all of us living one story, one aching version of humankind.

I was racing through his novel, whereas my mother had been stuck on the same page of her book for days, maybe weeks. I was devouring Naseem's manuscript, perhaps looking for Fouad. There was no mention of him. Was that odd? Hadn't they been friends? Naseem – who carried his devastated, paralysed father to Turkey and then on to Germany – said he lost his memory, that his life stopped in mid-2011. That events move so quickly he can't take them all in.

Was he in love with someone else when he left? I didn't ask. I didn't ask him questions any more. The moment never seemed right. 'As if I had time for love,' he would've said disdainfully. That's what Naseem always said when I asked him that question. He'd respond, half distracted and half irritated, implying that he didn't have time to shower, much less fall in love. 'I don't have time for love!' He never felt bad about giving an answer like that. Never dismissed the idea of infidelity by telling me I was enough for him or that he loved me, but on the grounds that he didn't have time to cheat! Was infidelity a matter of free time?

He didn't ask me to go with him to Turkey or Germany. Of course he knew that my mother and I wouldn't leave Damascus until we had news of Fouad. Naseem was certain I wouldn't join him. But still, he didn't ask. This wouldn't surprise anyone who knew Naseem; he never said anything because it should be said. Never uttered a word he didn't mean, or anything he wasn't sure would come true. Naseem knew I wouldn't leave my mother alone. He knew I wouldn't cross the border before Fouad returned, whether alive or dead. So he couldn't ask me to go with him, or even show how much he wished I could. He just slapped his cheeks every time we spoke.

We were having a row, I don't remember why. The cause of our fights was often unclear. (Naseem never tells me when he's upset with me, or even alludes to his frustration. It accumulates, layer by layer, until he explodes. When that happens, a tremor ripples across his face, his eyes bulge and the knot between his brows vanishes. He gestures, angrily purses his lips. A snarl extends to his nose and the two lines descending from either side.) At any rate, we were fighting and I was exasperated. Whenever we fought, Naseem disappeared afterwards, as if he was driving me out of his life, exiling me right when everything was exploding. He often disappeared and cut me off completely, as if I had never existed at all. I'd call him again and again, and he'd hang up on me, or not even pick up. I felt so alone in those moments. And those moments were many.

I saw myself sitting with him. Every bit of him was there, all his bones, everything about him. All of it, filling him up. I felt certain I knew what he was feeling, as if he were part of me. This was a different Naseem. He had the same face and clothes, left the same scent on my skin. But it was another Naseem, different from the one with whom I was fighting. This Naseem was as delicate as the breeze. He reached a loving hand to my face and gently brushed my cheek; he stroked my hair and tucked a strand behind my ear. I felt secure, safer than I'd ever felt in my life. A sense of tranquillity settled into my soul. I gazed into his eyes and complained about Naseem. But *he* was Naseem! It was like my dream, where I was driving a car and sitting next to myself. I complained about the Naseem I was fighting with, the one who so cruelly disappeared, to the compassionate Naseem sitting in front of me, there in a place I didn't recognise. It saddened Naseem that I felt so wronged. I saw his large, bright eyes fill with sorrow, and something flickered in them. He reached out to take me in his arms, all of me, the entirety of me that he chased away when we fought; he pulled me to his chest and hugged me. I was stunned by the tenderness flowing from his arms, it caught hold of me and swelled over me, and I wouldn't have cared if my life had ended right there, drowning in that embrace.

But I woke up a few seconds after he let go, still holding his warmth in my ribcage. I cried feverishly, wishing I could find that other Naseem. I didn't want a different man; I wanted a different Naseem, like the one in my dream.

Naseem's manuscript

I was fourteen, and it was a Friday. It was around that time that I began to hate Fridays. Of course this did not mean I liked school days – I hated those too. My hatred for school days was surpassed by my hatred for Fridays, however. On that first day of the weekend, the traffic abated, the voices of passers-by and neighbours grew softer, and the pace of social engagements slowed. One particular Friday, everyone was sleeping or confined to the house, restless and bored. I sat in my room, finishing my schoolwork, which was tiresome as always and only made Fridays feel lonelier. I heard Baba call me. I rushed into his room, which was adjacent to mine. He told me to sit on the edge of the bed, next to him. He was looking out the window, through the wooden shutters that chirped in the harsh winter wind. 'Look at that woman, lying naked on her daybed,' he said to me. I turned to the window with a start, shocked at the thought of a woman lying around naked in our neighbourhood, unconcerned by the gaze of her conservative neighbours. I didn't see her. I pressed him, and he pointed her out for me. 'Look there, in the window across from ours.' The window in the building across from ours was covered by an ancient screen that had been warped over time by the cold, heat, dry spells, rain and snow. Baba saw a naked woman on a daybed in the curves of the warped screen! He was imagining her. I was terrified. I smiled and mussed his hair. It was soft, now that the chemotherapy had stolen all the black strands from among the grey. I kissed his neck, on that small spot which my heart expanded to fill. I slipped back to my room, leaving Baba to frolic with his imaginary women.

I had long been jealous of every woman who crossed our threshold. They sat as close to my father as possible on our long white sofa. Sitting near him was not enough for me; I stuck so close it must have been bothersome. But he never once became cross with me. Never sighed or asked me to give him a bit more space. He would hug me, and I would occasionally lean in to kiss him, while the women sat nearby, clearly annoyed. That was how it felt, at any rate. And they annoyed me, too. I desperately wanted them to go, from the house and from our lives, for ever. Not only was Baba unbothered by the way I clung to him, this envious streak of mine amused him. He encouraged my jealousy. After the women left, he would watch me with strange satisfaction while I imitated them, making fun of the way they spoke, the colour of their clothes or even how they did their hair. I called them stupid, insensitive, brainless and horrid, while he quietly looked on and smiled.

One time when he went to Paris for medical treatment with my mother, I stayed with some family friends who had three daughters around my age. While I was there, another friend of my father's named Safeyya phoned their house and asked me to spend Friday with her. We could cook and watch a film; it would be fun. I was eleven at the time. I didn't like her because I knew that she and my father had dated before he married my mother. I didn't like how she was kind to me or how she tried to get close to me, because I knew it was just a way of getting close to my father. Children's emotions are raw, and not subtle.

Safeyya arrived at our friends' house to walk me over. I hated her blue eyes and blonde hair, maybe because she resembled my aunt and her daughters, who always teased me for my brown skin. We walked back to her place and it took nearly half an hour. I did like her apartment. Her living room had originally had high ceilings and she had divided it into two storeys. The new living room was on the bottom, and if you climbed up a short ladder you reached her bedroom, with a real wooden floor. I remember she made pasta with tomato sauce, minced meat and pine nuts. We ate lunch in her little kitchen, and then sat in the living room. I told her I thought her house was pretty, and that I wished I had my own upper bunk to hide in. She smiled and asked me a question that seemed odd. 'Do you want the ceiling to be colourful, and covered with stickers and drawings?' I said yes. Then she said, 'But if you cover the ceiling with pictures, paintings and colours, and lie in bed at night staring at the drawings, it will ruin your imagination.'

A few minutes later, the doorbell rang. It was not yet three in the afternoon. Safeyya opened the door. Her boyfriend was standing there, holding a small bouquet of flowers. He kissed her, and she let him in. He shook my hand, coolly. I could tell how irritated he was by my presence. He had expected to arrive and find his girlfriend alone. As soon as Safeyya sensed his annoyance, she looked at me and said, with a mix of tenderness and wickedness, 'We've had so much fun together, haven't we! Now go on, sweetie, you know your way home, right?'

I was a child of eleven. I had never left the house without my mother or father. I did not even know the names of the different neighbourhoods in the city. But on that epic afternoon, I decided to make my way back by myself. Safeyya had not given me the chance to say that I would not be able to manage it on my own, nor had she cared that it was her responsibility to take me to our friends' house. I went out into the street. I don't remember whether I felt scared. But a vast loneliness settled into my soul; I missed Mama and Baba terribly, and my longing for them began thumping within my ribcage. I started down the road, trying to find my way. And then all of a sudden I was lost. I went into a little shop and asked the owner if I could use the telephone. I kept a phone book in my head, where I memorised numbers for us, my aunt, my grandmother's house in the village and our friends, whom I called, and asked the shopkeeper his address so they could come and take me home.

This was the first thing Baba and I spoke about when he arrived home from Paris. I saw anger stir in his chest and ascend to cloud his beautiful eyes. He hugged me tenderly. And he never spoke to Safeyya again. He cut her off completely, because she had left his daughter to find her way back alone, to a house whose address she did not know. I was glad.

The second thing was something my father told me. He asked me to make him a cup of coffee, and announced that he had three months left. I remember exactly how he said it. *We still have three months together.*' 'Still', as if three months were three years. Now I feel certain it *was* three years. Father knew time would slip through our fingers like water, but he also knew how to take advantage of the time we still had. He prepared for the future. He'd been by my side for all of my eleven years, and would be with me for the years that lay ahead. He would be with me for those last three years, and what now amounts to more than twenty. I swallowed my tears that night and tried to understand, and then we agreed that three months was not much time at all.

We agreed that he would not pass away before the three-month mark, or even right after; we agreed that he would fight to stay beside me. And I believed him. The thought of his passing was incomprehensible. I was convinced he would not leave me. But despite my conviction, I lived those three years on death's razor edge. From morning until night, I walked in the shadow of fear. It took shape in my mind, as its features slowly gained definition ... until I was twenty-eight, and awoke one morning with arrhythmic heartbeats, a tightness in my chest and panic attacks that lasted all day.

This was fear. Kamil told me it was fear. Fear of losing someone grows in your soul, but you never notice it until it reaches a certain size. It sprouts hands and feet. Gains eyes and begins to stare at you, though still invisible itself. Races through your veins, though you never feel its footfall until it appears as a panic attack. And if the soul grows weak, fear invades the body instead. It meddles with your heartbeat. Steals sensation from your extremities. Makes your hands go numb. Snags your breath in your chest, until you choke and flail and feel you are drowning. Dizzies and blinds you, until you cannot think of anything but fear. This was fear. I was often afraid as a child. Fear is all I remember.

* * *

The final exam for elementary school, the brevet, was about a month and a half away. We stopped going to class in order to prepare. There were so many books I had to memorise 'from cover to cover', as we said. I went to stay with my father's cousin, her officer husband and their children. Their house was spacious, but every evening it constricted around me until I could hardly breathe. Shami Hospital, which was near the house, felt a world away. I called my mother every hour to check on her, and her voice, though weary, remained bright until the end. The family gave me my own room so I could study in peace, away from the commotion the grandchildren made. There were four of them, and then six when their grown-up daughter came to Damascus to visit from Europe, where she lived with her husband, another doctor.

Every morning I woke up in that room, where the balcony looked out on the homes of officers with a lower rank than our relative's husband. The decaying buildings were a terribly dreary sight. Their paint had deteriorated: dull blues, faded greens, and a yellow that had cracked with the passing seasons. The buildings looked like giant cement blocks stuck together, with apartments piled on top of each other and balconies all in rows. They depressed me so much that I kept the curtains drawn to protect myself.

One hot morning in May I opened my eyes and got out of bed. I did not call Mama like usual. Instead, I got out the youngest daughter's tape recorder, turned on some music ('*Bamboleo*' by the Gypsy Kings), and started to cry. Every time the tape ended, I kissed it. From eight in the morning until eight that night, I did not leave the room. I did not respond when the family urged me to come out and eat. All I did that day was cry. Through my tears, I talked to Baba, begging him not to go and leave me alone. I reminded him what he had told me hundreds of times: 'Don't be scared, I'm here with you.' Don't leave me, I told him, and I was sure he could hear me. Then my tears dried, and I could shed no more. At eight o'clock, I lay down on the bed and nodded off. I opened my eyes at midnight to a pitch-black room. Hunger wrenched my stomach, fear shattered my nerves, pain gnawed at my joints. I walked to the kitchen and went to the freezer, where I kept a large metal spoon: I used it to soothe my swollen red eyes whenever I had been crying. I was fourteen years old, and deep down I still am.

Did her tears dry at source like my mother's? My father has also passed away, and my brother too. Was this girl me, living alone with a mother who suddenly aged when her tears dried up? As I read the manuscript, I wondered again about Naseem's motivation. Why did he make his narrator carry all of our stories? Wasn't my life enough for a novel? Why so much hardship?

I texted him and told him I missed him. Silence. I imagined him and his father sitting in a little room. He hears the phone buzz. He picks it up. Reads the message. Gazes into the distance. Puts the phone down. Struggles to type. Or can't find the words to respond.

When I saw Kamil, I told him that Naseem had changed, though I didn't mention him by name. The time I finally worked up the nerve to admit to Kamil that I was in a relationship with a 'fellow patient', he laughed at that phrase. I don't know why I admitted it: Naseem and I had both promised we wouldn't reveal the other's identity to Kamil. Was it because I felt so filled with grief and fear at losing Naseem too? Was I mourning my ability to preserve him as he was, whole, the way I knew him? As expansive as the earth, as tempestuous as the sea?

Kamil told me that Naseem hadn't changed. ('Am *I* the one who's changed?' I blurted out. He shook his head.) He told me that Naseem 'was always that way', and I thought about this for a long time. Kamil meant that I hadn't loved Naseem as he was, but as I wanted him to be. I invented a fantasy version of him, gave him imaginary characteristics, then fell in love. Was it a coincidence that I'd fallen in love with a doctor like my father? But I hadn't known Naseem was a doctor when I met him, I told Kamil irritably. When had I stopped imagining him? Why did I now feel like he'd changed? 'Fantasies fade with time,' Kamil responded. And as time passes, the need for a new fantasy arises. My illusion had been diffused by the passing years. Or perhaps Naseem, by the force of his reality, had destroyed what I'd imagined and brought me back to earth . . . in front of him, in his house, where I searched for him and found nothing but cold silence.

The last time we saw each other was one year, seven months and twenty days ago. I made him his favourite salad, with lettuce and apple. We opened a bottle of red wine. It feels like it could have been yesterday. He filled his plate with salad, then forcefully speared a piece of lettuce and apple, as if he were plunging his fork into stone. He began stabbing and stabbing; I felt the piercing in my chest. When the fork was filled with all it could hold, he shoved it into his mouth and began to move his jaws alarmingly fast, as if he'd entered a speed-chewing race. He grabbed his glass of wine and gulped it down like water, then gave me the side-eye, implying I should fill it again. I poured him more and he downed it in one go. Fatigue began creeping over me. His fork clattered against the glass plate, and my hands went slack, as if I were the one wielding it, not Naseem. I watched in confusion as he continued his battle with the plate of salad. His jaw moved up and down, chewing the lettuce and apple with the ferocity of someone gnawing at a strip of meat. I felt exhausted. I heard a slow wheeze escape from my chest. Naseem's eyes were fastened on the plate in front of him. He didn't look at me until after he'd speared the last piece with his fork. I told him I was hurting, but I couldn't tell where the pain was. It wasn't a physical pain, like a headache or stomach ache, a sore hand or tired heart. This was deeper, as if something had welled up from my soul and begun coursing through my veins. Naseem nodded, signalling that he had heard me.

When I realised that Naseem wasn't going to ask me to go away with him, I begged him not to leave me. He never said, as the father in his novel says dozens of times to his daughter: 'I won't leave you. I'll stay with you.'

Naseem said nothing. Maybe because he wasn't my father. Maybe because he'd lost a parent. He gave me the key to his house and left. He told me I could come and go whenever I wanted. That made me feel secure: I get attached to places. If I possessed the key to his house, I thought that meant I possessed him. Or at least that I wouldn't lose him. It was our house now, and I had the key. Naseem left it empty instead of selling or renting it, and now the house, ready for his return, was mine. Even then I didn't know that houses meant nothing to Naseem, that he might forget there was a house waiting for him in the Italian quarter. The same neighbourhood where, in his novel, Saffeya lived, the woman who politely kicked a girl out of her home to spend time with her lover.

Suddenly I felt jealous. Did Naseem know his narrator? Were they close? Was he cheating on me and stealing my stories to hide his infidelity? He'd not only left me his house, but everything in it too. He had left his papers and notebooks and photographs, his memories, himself. Naseem had managed to let go of all his memories at once. Didn't he realise I was going to miss him, that my curiosity and longing would lead me to look through his notebooks and papers? Didn't he think of my feelings? Or did he trust that I wouldn't go near them? Perhaps the worst part was how certain he must have been that I wouldn't touch them, or even be interested. Or maybe he thought that if I discovered what I did by snooping through his things, he would be relieved of the burden of telling me. 'Take it . . . read it . . . then decide whether you would have stayed with me.' That's what I imagined him saying to me, again and again, and it brought the thought of losing him sharply back. *He* wasn't lost; *I* was the one who had lost him. I lost him the moment I opened his desk drawer, the moment I began reading his journals and papers and looking through his photographs.

So many photos of women, ranging in age from their twenties to their forties. They were carefully arranged in neat stacks. (I don't know whether Naseem had a system for sorting them. Alphabetically by name? Or by date of their relationship, the first to the most recent, or vice versa? Or according to how attached he was to them? It didn't matter.) Envy seared through me; I felt its flame pass through my stomach, rise to my chest and then my throat. I studied the faces. Naseem was with them in some of the photographs; others appeared alone. I looked away, and the searing sensation shot through my fingertips. I took a deep breath. I rummaged agitatedly through my purse. I went to the kitchen and poured myself a glass of water from the fridge, then swallowed half a Xanax. I'd stocked the fridge as if I were living there, or as if Naseem might return any day. I avoided his bedroom, with the open drawer and his things across the floor. I went into the living room and sat on the sofa where we'd often been together. I sat on his side of the sofa, as if by doing so I could draw some of his cold stoicism into my own body and breathe normally again.

I was short of breath now, but it hadn't prevented me from noticing certain details in the photos. I tried to shut my eyes and get rid of what I'd seen, but in vain. Cruel memory! If only we could sift through it to erase certain images and feelings, like a computer. Was his nameless narrator one of these women? I was angry that there were no pictures of me! But where would he have got one – we'd never taken a picture together because Naseem hated photographs and memories, at least that's what he'd told me more than once. If you hate photographs, Naseem, why the need to pose for so many with these other women? Then, from the depths of my panic, a kind of joy emerged. I don't know where it came from: how can panic give birth to joy? I thought about it. His past had always been so hazy to me, but the photos I'd held in my hands a few minutes earlier had brought a glimpse of it, at least, into focus.

The half Xanax, small and rosy-hued, began flowing through my veins, rising to my head and leaving a fragile sense of reassurance in its wake. I took a deep breath, and tried to stay calm. I went back to his room. I sat cross-legged on the floor next to the drawer and the photographs and picked them up again. I gazed into those eyes, so still it felt like they were gazing back at me, like they might emerge from the photograph to draw even closer to my own, to stare into my eyes even as they brimmed with fear (to use Kamil's phrase). But there was something about Naseem's expression. It was always exactly the same! As if all the photos had been taken at the same moment, just with different outfits and different women. His gaze was distant, indifferent, drifting from one empty space into another, as if it belonged nowhere. Wouldn't love have made him a different person every time – or did he keep his soul shuttered in?

I felt the jealousy burrow deeper and deeper. I hadn't known anything about these women, all different ages, different kinds of beautiful, different eyes and skin colour. I envied Naseem's stoicism, indifference and ability to let go, as if nothing existed beyond his own body. As if everything else were a separate planet that meant nothing to him at all. What made this being so removed from his surroundings? Was he the father in the story? Didn't he resemble him? Had the woman who inspired Naseem's novel loved him because he was like her father, a distant writer?

And for myself, do I love you because you resemble my father, a doctor who was afraid of fear?

Naseem's manuscript

I was fourteen years old . . . and still am. The doorbell rang at my father's cousin's house. I do not
remember whether anyone else was awake – I cannot recall for sure. When I think of that scene, I see
only myself, sitting in their house, and my father,
lying in a bed in room 203. I crossed the short distance from the freezer, where the spoon was, to the
front door. Firm steps, obscured by a haze of anxiety. I opened the door. A family friend was standing
there. She looked tired. She kissed me neutrally, a
normal kiss as if it were a normal day. She said nothing, and I asked no questions. There was no need for
words. She remained standing at the front door and
I headed to the room I had just exited. I dressed
quickly. Tied back my long hair as I always did. Put
on my shoes. And left with her. The taxi was waiting
for us out front. Ever gentle, she did not utter a word
the whole way there, from the house at the end of

Mezzeh Highway to Shami Hospital. I looked out the window at the illuminated streets, and was surprised to see that the traffic lights were still working. They shone green, then orange, then red. I thought life would stop when it happened. Traffic lights would stop changing, cars would freeze in the streets, and everyone in this huge city would retreat into their homes and disappear behind walls. There would be nothing but silence.

I was fourteen years old . . . and still am . . . and I knew! Had I not spent the whole day drying my tears and begging him not to go? We arrived at the hospital. We went up to the second floor and walked down a corridor that looked the same as it had for years. But it wasn't the same. It was packed with friends. They greeted me silently. They looked at me with glistening eyes, as if they were gazing into the distant past. Was the past that long ago? The past was just a few hours ago, Baba! Was I the only one still in this distant past? I searched for news of him in their eyes and looked around for my mother. I couldn't see her. I remember being pushed firmly towards room 203. I said nothing. I fought back. I said I did not want to go in. I could not bear to see his body. How could a being so full of life become just a body, with eyes that stared into endless space? Then the walls vanished; I imagined him lying in the hospital room. Mama was with him. She asked the doctor to give them a few minutes. She washed his body, while singing him his favourite song: 'Oh how under the howdah, oh how we embraced . . .'

'Where's Mama?' I asked fearfully. (I could not handle them both passing away on the same day; I had never imagined I could survive even one of them dying.) Mama emerged from the room. She had finished whatever she was doing and handed her husband's body to Dr Soufjan, entrusting him to the medical team and their lonely procedures. Slowly, she walked down the narrow corridor. Her eyes were swollen with tears. (Grief stretched over everything, like a web, and many years later it is still with me, because I am fourteen still. I could not grow up. Could not leave the corridor on the second floor: my soul is still suspended there, in that tunnel.) Mama came up to me. She hugged me. I could not make the tears come. I tried. And failed. I hugged her, trying to envelop her, her whole skinny, feeble body sapped by fatigue. 'It's over.' Those were the only two words I caught between her tears: 'It's over.'

We went home that night to a house we had not lived in for nearly a month. We entered cautiously. A vacant house, empty of life and the lives we had lived there. Then everyone else left, and my mother and I were alone.

We could not find words. The silence arched over our heads, filled with sorrow. Only two heads now, not three. We went into their bedroom. It was past three in the morning. We laid down next to each other in his bed, and slept for an hour, maybe two. I don't remember.

When we woke again, suddenly, we did not speak. Mother went into the kitchen to make coffee. I was in the living room, opening shutters that had been closed for months. Our first-floor neighbour was hanging clothes out to dry in her little garden. Her lips stretched into a smile when she saw me. 'How's the Mister?' she asked. I smiled back and replied, 'He passed.' I still had not shed a single tear.

I went into my room. Closed the door. The atmosphere in the house was different. Not even my room was the same: it felt like the waiting room in an airport or train station. I looked in the mirror and did not see my reflection – only my father staring back at me. 'How could you leave me?' I asked. 'Can you hear me? Help me cry.' But he did not. I put on the black clothes my mother had told me to buy a few days earlier. The loose fabric felt like gravel on my skin. The house began to fill with friends. All I remember from that day was the rush of people and friends filling every room. I remember my mother sitting and wailing, her eyelids swollen with a weariness that had been building up for years, their skin faintly blue like the open sky. I remember glimpsing her pure exhaustion that day, brimming up and streaming from her eyes. And from this well of weariness, my mother drew strength. She tried to steel herself, and only relaxed when a deluge of tears fell down her face.

And me? How could I walk through life without him? How could I live without him next to me in his bed, without kissing his neck and telling him everything that came to mind? How could I live, who would I be, without him? How could he go and leave me? The huge void in my soul – what could fill it?

(How can I breathe without going into your room on tiptoe to count your breaths, to check that you are still breathing? Am I still breathing? 'You won't grow up until you're able to say that he's dead . . .' Kamil tells me. 'Your father didn't pass away . . . he died.')

A certain insouciance, I realised, was beginning to drift up from beneath the pain. My fear of death was gone, because my greatest fear had come true. No more need for sleepless nights, afraid of him leaving me. Now he was gone, and I was alone. No more need to fear fear. I had lived my whole childhood afraid of fear, of walking behind his coffin, averting my eyes from where he lay wrapped in a white shroud, sleeping in a hole just big enough for his body. A hole that was not big enough for me too. When the funeral was over, when night had fallen and we arrived back home, that was when I began to cry. Tears poured from my eyes. I called out for my mother. She came. She held me. I threw myself into her arms, trying to absorb her warmth, trying to catch my breath, which had been lost with his.

The house changed; it began to take different forms. It even smelled different. In the beginning, his passing (I refuse to say 'death', and I hear Kamil banging his head against the wall, but I do not want to grow up) became a source of conflict for my mother and me. We were lost, alone, clutching painful memories in our souls, and pain beyond anything a body could hold. At first we did not know how to be without him. He had been our reason for living, the engine of our projects and imaginations. Now we were alone in a house so bitter and cold, fighting over every little thing, unable to make sense of our lives and continue. Nothing was the same, and we could not go on as normal. But we persevered. We continued this battle for nearly two years without reaching a truce, until finally we tired and both surrendered.

Over time, we came to terms with our loneliness. We learned to deal with it without fighting, and to love each other again. For so many years we had focused only on loving him. I know I was often combative or passive-aggressive. For the first two years, my mother's presence in the house just reminded me of my father's absence. I was rude to her, as if punishing her for his passing. I would tell her something the way I would have told him, and then blame her for not having his patience or responding as he would have done. I had no compassion for her loss, and did not think about her sadness. I was preoccupied with my own. I had no empathy for her pain, as if I were the only one dealing with grief. But then I would feel terribly guilty, apologise and make a miserable attempt to demonstrate how much I loved and needed her.

Showing my feelings for my mother did not come easily to me. I often sat across from her and gazed at her sad face, looking into her eyes and concentrating on what to say, but then the words crumbled and their meaning disintegrated. I was unable to express my thoughts. Words became dirt in my mouth, so I stayed silent. And before long I would again be struck with remorse and make another awkward attempt – because surely if I made such an effort to say something, love would sprout anew – but when my words emerged, they sounded as manufactured and formulaic as a composition lesson from school.

Physically I was a girl of fourteen, but my soul had matured into its thirties. It is so hard when one's soul outpaces one's body, slipping away at the beginning of the day, growing up on its own and developing new characteristics, only to be forced to return each night to inhabit the same body. No matter how much I leaped and flailed, pretended, rebelled, I could find no other home for my soul than my still-young body.

To my mother, I was simply fourteen. It was as if all the years Baba had packed into the short time he had left had somehow eluded her.

My mother had, in crucial ways, been absent. She had become obsessed with reading about nutrition and strengthening the immune system, and with her phone, which connected her to the world, from America to China to Japan to Korea to France. When she heard about a new type of treatment discovered abroad, she began searching for a way to obtain whatever nutritional or medicinal substances or plants they were. She had been attached to his body, not his soul; concerned with saving his body so that it could still house his soul. What use was the soul if the body could no longer go on? I, on the other hand, I was attached to his soul. We soared through time together, flying past the thresholds of twenty, then thirty years old. We grew up together, even though he had passed on.

My fourteen-year-old body held a thirty-year-old soul, and my mother did not realise at all. She might not even have known that I had turned fourteen. Once, we were walking in the street together through our bustling neighbourhood, alongside the narrow pavement. I was holding her hand, as if I were her mother. Suddenly, she looked at me and said, 'Hey, little Mama, step down from the pavement. Walk next to me.' I had not been walking on the pavement. My hand was higher than hers, so she must have thought I was on the pavement, a step higher than her! She had not noticed that I had grown older and taller. I was one step taller than her, a step in time.

So, the house became a prison and I never missed an opportunity to escape. I returned to our cousin's house, and the room where I had left my soul in tears that day. I stayed with them and left my mother, not thinking about what she would do all day, alone. I figured she was used to my absence. After that I went to stay with another cousin and her husband. Then – it was maybe three years after my father had passed – I became sick and stopped going to school. There was not a doctor in Damascus my mother didn't take me to. Not an X-ray or MRI she did not have performed. But they showed nothing. She was beside herself. How could *nothing* incapacitate me for days? My headaches were so vicious that I beat my head against the wall. I lost consciousness again and again. My extremities shook and my tongue trembled, and I lost the ability to stand or speak.

One time I was at my aunt's apartment on the eleventh floor. I went out onto the balcony, sat on the green balustrade, and dangled my feet off the edge. I stared at the street far below and at the passers-by, so small from that towering height, and thought about throwing myself off. I was not nervous or afraid. I did not start to sweat or think of my mother. I didn't even imagine my body falling from the eleventh floor, flailing awkwardly in the air, then finally colliding with the asphalt where it would burst. I didn't consider whether I would still be alive when I hit the ground, if I would feel pain on impact. Did not think about what it would mean to throw myself off, for it all to be over in the space of seconds. I just thought that the moment had come for me to join my father. I thought he was waiting for me, that we would spend the rest of time together. My soul was in my thirties, and he was still fifty-five: he had stopped ageing the day he passed. Both of us were where we had been when his soul departed, he in room 203, and I in my room at our cousin's house.

'It's delayed grief.' That's what the doctor had said after a lengthy examination of my brain and nervous system. I was grieving now, after years of denial. Suddenly, I had understood that Baba had passed away, and that evading that truth was not working any more. I grieved when I chose to: at first I had not accepted that he was gone. He had passed away too young, not at the time we agreed upon. And I did not believe it. Three years later I was exhausted, and finally began to mourn. I had fainting spells, and that persistent, terrible headache. My extremities trembled, my tongue went numb, and I tried to kill myself, not with the goal of dying, but to prove to myself that I could go when I wanted to, that I controlled my own fate. I wanted to prove that remaining alive was a choice too, and not a bad one, until I decided the opposite.

I had started to believe that death would ease my anxiety and bring me peace. When I thought about losing someone close to me and panicked, I told myself there was no need to be afraid. If they passed away, all I had to do was end my life and I would find peace. As I was sitting on the green balustrade, dangling my feet in the air, Mama Vic walked into the room and saw me. I had called Aunt Victoria 'Mama Vic' since I first learned to speak. She came in and did not seem surprised to see me sitting on the balustrade on the eleventh floor, my feet hanging over the edge. She smiled calmly. I do not know where she found such serenity; she was known for being blunt, quick-tempered and vociferous. She walked up to me. Didn't touch me. She just asked me, gently, to come with her to the living room. Lunch was ready. We went down together and didn't speak of it, as if I hadn't been about to jump from the eleventh floor a few seconds earlier. Later I learned that a neighbour had called Mama Vic, her joints trembling with fear, and told her how at that very moment a girl was trying to leap from her balcony.

Death was salvation, one way or another. Not just death, but the idea of it too. The sense of control over my own fate at a terrible moment in life felt liberating; it made me lighter. What good was life without death? What good was death without a soul, thrumming and glowing in the body?

What would happen if she ended her life? I began to hope that she would. But soon I realised that if she did end her life, we likely wouldn't know. I sat reading the manuscript late into the evening and began to wonder, if the young woman committed suicide, whether that would prevent Naseem from doing the same, whether her death could cure his own fixation. Naseem's eyes were trained on death; he gazed into it; it walked along-side him everywhere. A few years before it actually happened, he told me how his mother and sister would die. I was shocked by his detailed description, and I believed him. There wasn't anyone in his family he didn't kill with words, describe their funeral, and come to terms with losing, again and again and again.

Why did the girl in his novel choose to delay her grief at her father's passing? How did she become someone who could stand on the other bank of life? While she delayed her mourning, Naseem was running laps around her. I remember one time when we spent the night at his house and he told me all these stories about death. How his mother had been on her way back from visiting a friend who had lost her only son and was starting to go senile. His mother couldn't comprehend that her best friend was losing her memory – even though the friend asked her how Naseem's grandmother was doing, when she had died many years earlier. Then the friend got confused and didn't recognise her any more. She thought Naseem's mother was her own sister, who had also passed away years earlier. 'How are you, Sis? How're the kids?' She spoke like this for a whole hour. Naseem's mother left her oldest friend's house feeling flustered and upset. She was so agitated that she didn't notice a massive lorry hurtling down the road as she crossed. She didn't even hear its horn blare. The lorry driver couldn't slow down fast enough and he hit her.

I asked Naseem how he knew all these details. How did he know she'd been at her friend's house, and what she had been feeling when she left? How did he know that his mother's friend had thought she was her sister? He said his mother's friend had told him. But when I pressed him further, asking how a woman who had lost her memory remembered what they had spoken about, Naseem gave in and admitted that the part about his mother leaving her friend's house flustered was made up. Later I discovered the whole story was a fiction: his mother was still alive. He also killed his sister and mourned her death. He killed his father and grieved, and then came to terms with his own death. That's where things ended.

He died too.

Naseem's manuscript

I missed a whole year of school when I was sick. It was the final year before our graduation exams. My mother gave the school a medical report from the neurologist, who had determined that I could not attend class due to a nervous breakdown: I was experiencing sudden losses of consciousness and trembling in my extremities. (A few years later, the same kind of report would be given as proof of my eldest cousin's insanity, in order to secure her release from the secret police. She had marched into the polling station and voted 'No' on the referendum, rejecting Bashar al-Assad's succession to power.) I began studying at my father's cousin's house, always in the same room as before. I only went to school to sit the necessary exams.

Since the school bus did not go all the way to our relatives' house, they had their driver take me to school in their Mercedes. Each time we approached the main entrance in Nejmeh Square, I begged him to drop me off far from the gate, afraid that someone might see me getting out of a Mercedes with tinted windows. My knees trembled and I blushed; I felt that a Mercedes was embarrassing. My father had taught me, though without ever saying so directly, that our little family was right when it came to cars. All the families of my friends at school owned a car, sometimes more than one. We did not. Secretly, I felt that they were the exception and we were the rule. So what if this car was a Mercedes? I got out far from the main gate, crossed the street and quickly walked the rest of the way to school.

At the front office, the receptionist greeted me cordially, though not without a certain condescension, as if welcoming a new patient to the mental ward. She told me to sit behind her desk and gave me the exam, which had been printed for me in advance. I answered all the questions and left. I was careful not to run into any friends in the long corridor between the office and the classrooms, or on the stairs leading to the main gate.

I looked for Ali, the driver, and saw that he had parked far from the gate, as I had asked him to do. Ali took care of every task you could imagine. He cleaned the house, which was at least 500 square metres, top to bottom. He cooked for them, even on his days off. He did the shopping daily, sometimes several times a day. But the daughters of the family were cruel to him. They were constantly shouting at him or boasting in front of him. Their other driver, Ammar, was from Aleppo, not Tartus, and thus 'more distinguished' in their eyes. They were always careful not to annoy him or overburden him with too many tasks and errands. They spoke gently to him. Ammar was more refined than Ali – 'svelte' was their description. His cologne filled the car when he drove. A 'gentleman', they said in English; he opened the door for them, unlike Ali, who stayed in his seat behind the wheel. His voice was calm and composed, not like Ali's. Personally, I think they were afraid of him! But I never understood why they feared people from Aleppo and dismissed those from Tartus.

The eldest daughter was alluringly beautiful, with big, bright eyes. She married a young Sunni man from Damascus, and whenever he visited the whole family dressed up as if going out. When they welcomed their son-in-law into their home, they wore their fanciest shoes, never house slippers. He may only have seen them in pyjamas once in his life! Even when he spent the night at their house with their daughter and wore shorts and an undershirt himself, they always dressed to the nines. They would not put on pyjamas until their bedroom doors were shut for the night, and they did not emerge the next morning until they were fully dressed! When they invited him to lunch, they sat at the formal dining table. They used gold-rimmed plates that only saw the light a few times a year, during feasts to which they invited 'eminent' official figures. They laid out a full table setting, with two sets of forks and knives and embroidered cloth napkins, and they piled food on fancy platters which they presented fresh and hot. When the meal was done, they sat in the living room reserved for guests and served tea in delicate glass cups, not forgetting the sweets and fruit that rounded off proper hosting etiquette. They asked him about the engineering projects he supervised, and spoke about current affairs, prices, the economy, American and Russian foreign policy, the Cold War, Afghanistan, Europe, and the politics of countries near and far – any country except Syria. There was nothing about Syria to discuss. No one ever brought up politics, though it lurked in everyone's mind.

Their other son-in-law was the son of an important officer from the Ghab Plain, and they were not afraid to host him in their pyjamas and slippers. With him they always ate in the kitchen, serving food straight from the pot onto plates with the occasional chipped edge. They might not even formally serve him, but let him do it himself. He was 'practically family', they said, not a stranger or guest. They spoke informally with him, and did not serve tea. They discussed family matters in front of him, and never skipped their daily nap on account of his presence. When he left they did not wish him goodbye; his absence was hardly noticed. They did not intentionally treat him so differently. It was not as if they had all agreed in advance that when their Damascene in-law arrived, they would wear formal clothes and sit at the dining table reserved for guests. Their actions were unconscious. When they decided to visit their daughter who was married to the man from the Ghab Plain, they never told her they were coming. If it occurred to them to visit, they got in the car and drove to her villa. If she was not at home, they let themselves in and waited for her; since the development where she lived had plenty of guards, the doors were always open. Meanwhile, a visit to their other daughter required prior arrangement, consent and significant notice. They dressed in their finest to visit her, and brought sweets, fruit, chocolate and citrus juice, as if they did not want her to go hungry, or as if she were living in a prison, not the neighbourhood of Mezzeh. And every time they visited her, they asked before leaving whether she wanted anything, as if she was in constant need.

My father's relative's family was loving and kind. They accommodated my sorrows and always accepted my depression and fear. They tried hard, all of them, to make up for his passing, without understanding, perhaps, that no one can fill that emptiness, not even by a drop; that it only expands as days, and then years, go by. I learned that in the face of loss, the soul defends itself by cramming the void with whatever it can. It chases after details, even the smallest (and often most superficial) ones, holds tight to whatever it can find. Eventually, the soul realises the void is vast and bottomless, that the hole ripped in one's memory cannot be mended. And that it is drowning.

I hated them as a family. I loved everyone individually but preferred not to be with them all together. Maybe family gatherings clouded my memories of spending time just Baba and me; soon enough, any big gathering was enough to stoke my fears. I would only be with people one on one. If there was a large get-together and I was obliged to attend, I would single someone out and strike up a conversation to one side. I didn't hate 'family' as an idea, it was more that the word meant very little to me now. Aside from my grandmother Khadija, I had no close relatives left on my father's side: no aunts dear to my heart, no uncles, no grandfather. The one uncle I was fond of had passed away. My grandmother was all I had left.

My mother's extended family was rather small, not really a family in the true sense of the word. Sometimes I felt her relatives were mythical: not because they did not exist, but because I knew them more through stories than through experience. I would listen to my mother and aunt recount family tales and imagined the people in them. My grandmother Helena was a Turkish Christian. She fell in love with a Christian man in Turkey and gave birth to my Aunt Victoria (Mama Vic). Then her husband passed away and she met a Syrian who told her that his name was Joseph. She assumed he was Christian. He asked her to marry him, so she left Turkey and came with him to Damascus. There she found out he was Muslim: his name was actually Youssef. But this changed nothing for her, and they were married. Together they had my mother and uncle, and the children grew up Muslim. Mama Vic, who was Christian, also married a Muslim and had two children.

I remember my maternal grandfather's house in the neighbourhood of Afeef. It was a typical Damascene house with three storeys, and each floor had a space open to the sky. When my grandmother passed away, my grandfather began sleeping on the ground floor, so he would not have to go up and down the stairs. On the ground floor was the kitchen, dining room, living room, sitting room (which became my grandfather's bedroom when he fell ill) and a little toilet. On the second floor was a large toilet and the 'sunroom', which was filled with plants and flowers. On the third floor were three bedrooms: one for my aunt, one for her older brother, my uncle, and one for her youngest daughter.

My aunt's husband died young . . . but I'm losing track now. (Do I actually remember him, or have I recreated him in my imagination from the pictures my aunt and cousins saved?) When my aunt's husband passed away, she and their younger daughter moved in with my grandfather. The older daughter was studying in the Soviet Union, and only visited on holidays. When my grandfather passed away, my uncle married and his wife moved in. The happiest memories of my childhood took place in that house. It is where I first learned to walk, where I said my first words. It is where I often scaled the tall staircase that connected the courtyard to the green space dividing the two floors. I would walk up, sit on the top step and come back down, slowly at first, and then insanely fast. Then I would do it again.

When my grandfather passed away, my aunt bought a house in New Sham, a new development just west of Damascus. My uncle stayed in the family home with his wife, and then a few years later he decided to sell it. Someone from outside the neighbourhood bought the house, and he split the proceeds with my aunt.

I remember the last occasion that Mama and I visited the house. She stood in the courtyard, looked up at the third floor where the bedrooms were, and shouted at the top of her lungs, 'Mammaaaa . . . Mother!' It frightened me. I thought she had lost her mind. But I said nothing. She told me that she was calling for her mother in her childhood home one final time. She was saying goodbye to the house in her own way. The house felt like a mother to her, and she addressed her from the ground floor: 'Mammaaaa.' She wanted to hear her voice there before leaving. The house had been witness to so many family stories, and when it was no longer in our lives it was as if we had turned a well-loved page. As well as my grandfather's house, the houses on either side of his also disappeared from our lives. I had spent my childhood between three: Aunt Um Hanan's, Aunt Um Kamal's, and Teeti's. Teeti was a friend of my grandmother's, and she lived with her husband and their two daughters, Bidrea and Messika, both of whom I called aunt. My mother and her siblings had called Bidrea and Messika's mother 'Teeti' since they were little, and when I asked my mother what Teeti's real name was, she couldn't tell me! We left that house and all the houses in that neighbourhood, each filled with stories and a flood of memories . . . up to the brim.

Seven years ago, my mother heard that her childhood home was for sale again. She told me she wanted to buy it. She would sell her current house and reclaim her family home, the one that held both of our childhoods. My soul simmered with excitement. Minute by minute I counted the hours, as if waiting to meet my father, surprising me with his return. (This was my sole recurring dream at night: that suddenly my father was back and I was overwhelmed with an indescribable joy. It was a kind of joy I had never experienced in my waking life, a joy reserved especially for this dream, one I felt only at night, only when I saw him. We always decided to meet in a coffee shop, though it was one I had never actually been to, an imaginary coffee shop. My father would order a beer, even though he had actually preferred arak or whisky. Why this detail, I do not know! I would be drinking wine, trying to keep him in view, wanting him to stay, as if I knew it was all a dream. Then suddenly I would pause. Where should I start? So much had happened, too much to explain, and I didn't know how to tell him things, in what order, so as not to shock him by how much had changed.)

And so I went home with my mother, to the house that held our childhoods.

Naseem wrote about houses the way others might write about the soul. There was a paradoxical dissociation in his relationship to place. He told me that he never felt he belonged in any of the houses in which he had lived. He said this was a conscious choice, but also one that terrified him. He told me he always chose what terrified him. Being afraid of fear was a constant, awful state for him: it made him invent all kinds of ways to be frightened. He wanted to decide when the fear would strike him, rather than let it do so when he least expected.

Once he called me, out of breath. He was panting hard, his breathing was uneven. He told me that he'd been on his way home, and was still quite far away, when he got stuck in traffic and left the taxi because it had been so crowded and hot and he was afraid. He got out, only to be struck by more fear. His terror peaked and then vanished, as sweat streamed from every pore in his body. Naseem ran from the taxi and down the street in search of oxygen, but found only the searing sun, thick air, midday heat and his own ragged breath. He barely made it home, and was calling to tell me he had arrived. He had reached the tipping point of crisis, there, in his house, when he closed the door and shut out the heat and commotion.

Another time when we were chatting I told him that you feel you belong when you're at home. But he rejected the idea, claiming that there were very few places where he belonged. He explained that a house, to him, meant nothing. His room, for instance, *that* was where he felt a sense of belonging. But not even his room, just his low wooden bed. Then he began narrowing the scope and tried to convince me that he didn't feel he belonged in the whole bed, just on the right side where he slept. I smiled and teased him, saying that the right side of his bed was a vast expanse, he had to narrow it down. My joke didn't make him laugh, though, it just cinched the knot between his brows into a deeper scowl. I told him that what he'd experienced in the street was just a panic attack. He shook his head: no. He didn't believe in panic attacks. Or anything to do with interior worlds.

I found it surprising that he was seeing Kamil given that he didn't acknowledge his interiority. Naseem told me that the soul doesn't fail the body – *au contraire*. The way I understood panic attacks was that a weary soul burdens the body and its exhaustion is expressed in physical symptoms like shortness of breath and disorientation. But he didn't believe things worked that way. In his view, when the body becomes weary it heaves its weight on the soul. When the body tires, it tires the soul. If not, the soul could exist on its own. Why does the soul die when the body does? If the soul were cleaved from the body somehow, went mad and tried to kill itself, it wouldn't succeed if the body wasn't tired. A sound body is life. Is a sense of belonging. I told him that it was the soul that chose to commit suicide; the body just carried out the act. He told me that what I was saying proved him right. If the body wasn't ready to die, then a suicide attempt would be just that – an attempt. The body was what decided to stay or go. If it had hope, it would resist; if it despaired, it would submit.

I asked him if it was his body, or soul, that loved me. The body is what falls in love, he said. Eyes love, as do the ears, hands and mouth. Isn't it the mouth that tastes something and accepts or rejects it? Isn't it the stomach that throws up rotten food? Isn't it the ears that choose a certain kind of music? You're talking about taste, I told him, and taste pertains to the soul. He teased me. No, Naseem didn't acknowledge interiority. How would he deal with panic attacks if he didn't understand them? How would he find a sense of home or belonging if, as he claimed, his soul wasn't moved by smells, and his body was all that stayed or fled? Maybe Naseem held on to things that meant nothing to him. If I found strange things in his desk and dresser drawers, perhaps they were the only things that made him feel he belonged. His tipping points.

What was he doing now in Germany, I wondered, so far from the things to which he belonged? Had he stopped slapping his precious cheeks?

In his house I found piles of receipts he'd saved, from restaurants, coffee shops, clothing stores and supermarkets. I even found handwritten receipts, from fruit and vegetable carts, I think. I found a small box stuffed with tags from clothing he'd bought – he pulled off the tags showing the brand and price and saved them. I found corks from wine bottles. Loads and loads of empty medicine bottles, which he kept for reasons I didn't understand.

Then I found a neat stack of papers printed in black and white.

Obituaries!

An obituary for his father, another one for his mother, a third for his sister, and a fourth, fifth and sixth for people I didn't know. My vision blurred; suddenly I felt light-headed, and a chill shot from my neck to my knees. I found my obituary! Naseem had written an obituary for me, printed it and added it to the rest. He never told me he was anticipating my death. I knew he was anticipating his family's deaths and his own, but he'd never spoken to me about mine, even though he had clearly imagined it. I read my name, and the page trembled between my fingers. My name shook. I saw it move left and right, as if it wished to escape the page. I was scared. Not because I thought it was an omen; I didn't believe in signs. Because I knew that in his heart I was dead, just like his father and mother and sister.

'Knowledge is death,' Naseem once said to me. I contemplated the phrase, which could mean so many things. I hadn't wanted to ask and start a discussion that might open up big questions. I didn't like big questions when I was with him, and immersed myself in the small things.

Later, I realised that I loved him best when he was silent. As soon as he opened his mouth and began to speak, I felt a sense of aversion come over me. I didn't know why. When I told Kamil about it, he tried to hide a triumphant smile: my distaste whenever Naseem spoke was proof that I didn't love him as he was, but as I imagined him to be. When he was silent, my imagination kicked into gear, and when he spoke it ground to a halt. I thought about Naseem's words, though: 'Knowledge is death.' I knew that novelty impels us to explore. And when we know something well, it becomes something we can possess, and then lose.

I died when he got to know me well.

I took my obituary with me. I folded it carefully, the way Naseem folded his shirts and jumpers. (I used to watch, from a distance, how he took a cotton jumper and smoothed it distractedly, how the moment seemed to expand and then repeat, as if it were something from a past life, or déjà vu. He would lay the jumper on the table or bed, fold the sides in, then smooth it flat and fold it again. He would gently pick it up, lay it across his palms, carry it across the room and place it on a shelf in the closet, which looked more like a mother or grandmother's closet than one belonging to a man in his forties.)

Yes, I folded my obituary carefully and slipped it in my purse. Then I turned off the lights, shut the door and went home, where my mother was still reading her page 24. My little room had a narrow door that opened onto a small balcony full of plants and flowers. I headed to the solitary olive tree in the corner. I dug a hole by hand, and observed dirt collecting under my fingernails. I dug and dug. I buried the obituary there, then filled the hole with dirt and piled more dirt on top of it. I don't know why I buried the obituary instead of destroying it. Maybe I felt the act of destruction might somehow imbue it with life. I didn't want anyone to read it. Even if I tore it into pieces too small to read, fragments of words would inevitably survive. I didn't want anyone to lay eyes on a single letter, or touch a scrap of the paper. So I buried it and forgot about it. No. I didn't forget about it. Every time I went into my room and glanced at the olive tree, I imagined the paper suffocating under layers of dirt.

A few days later I had a nightmare and woke up in terror with my heart leaping in my chest, up towards my neck and down towards my legs. I was sitting in a tight space, not quite big enough for me. I had sat down and wrapped my arms around my knees, pulling them into my chest, as if hugging myself. My legs were bent and pressed against my chest and I hugged them; I could hardly breathe. I was covered in dirt, it filled my nostrils, eyes and ears, and felt damp against my skin. Despite that, I could see. Or maybe I couldn't, but it wasn't me in the dream. I was watching myself. I was outside that body, all folded and piled on top of itself. Is it true that the soul leaves the body at night and dreams alone? I was watching myself in the dream, suffocating, begging for air, squirming under the weight of the soft, moist dirt, thinking that even fresh dirt could become hard as stone if compacted. I was myself in the dream, and I was the paper, buried by the olive tree, on which was written my obituary. Then I saw my name engraved on my back, next to my date of birth. I didn't see my date of death recorded. I hadn't died, then? I wasn't the paper with the obituary in the dream? What was I?

I struggled to open my eyes. I thought about the tattoo. The one Naseem got done in late 2011. We'd been alone in his house, sitting next to each other, and he lifted his cotton jumper to reveal his back. Inked on his skin, I saw his name written in Arabic, alongside his date of birth, his address in Damascus, and the address of his family home in Homs. He told me he was afraid of dying in an explosion or under the shelling and becoming an unidentified body. Without time to identify him, or search for his family, he would be buried in the closest plot of land. I didn't say to him that if he died in an explosion or bombing, his body might be so mangled that his tattoo would be indecipherable, even if scraps or pieces of him with fragments of words were found. I wanted him to hold on to whatever could comfort him, even if it was an illusion.

Naseem's manuscript

My mother knocked on the door to the building. In that instant, an image from years earlier flashed across my mind. I saw her raise her head to the sky and shout: 'Mammaaaa . . . Mother!'

A woman in her seventies opened the door. She welcomed us in. My mother went first and I followed. A short, narrow corridor linked the door to the building and the inner courtyard. I was surprised by how small the courtyard was, barely big enough for my mother and me, with lots of doors leading to little rooms. With eager eyes I searched the house, the first place I had formed memories. I looked for the long staircase brushed hundreds of times by the hem of my clothing as I flew up and down. But all I found were a few steps, no more than ten. I scaled them quickly, in less time than the space between 'Mammaaaa . . .' and 'Mother . . .' The 'sunroom', which had been my playground as a child, was not there. All I found was a small space, just enough for a chair or two. There were three bedrooms, where I had sat on the bed or quietly played, whose combined area was no greater than my current bedroom. Where had our vast house gone? In losing it, I also lost that expansive period of my childhood.

The realisation that children measure places according to their small, fragile bodies surprised me! To my young self, the place had seemed huge; to my little legs, those few steps were a tall staircase and it took ages to descend them from top to bottom. The house's other distinctive features had been obscured by its new occupants. They had covered the floor with cheap, olive-coloured carpeting, and had painted the walls dull colours. The house looked ugly. Irredeemable. Restoring it to how it once was: impossible. We left, mournfully. My mother was sad because the house was no longer filled with her family or their stories and memories, which had slowly seeped away. The new residents' memories filled the place, as did their smells and the cells of their bodies, which drifted onto the sofa and walls and accumulated with the passing days. Just as in my aunt's house. The sofas were covered with layers of them, hard to get rid of.

My mother did not buy back her family home. She did not recover her childhood, not entirely. But she did recover part of it when she bought a house nearby, further down the same street. Her new house had three storeys, too. But we only spent one night there. This was at the beginning of the revolution, after we had sold our first home because we could not live there any more.

A few weeks before my father died, he asked my mother to call the lawyer and tell him to come to the hospital to put the house in my name. He did the same with the house in the village, where my grandmother still lives. It never felt like I owned a house, much less two: they did not feel like they were mine; I didn't even have the keys. I certainly didn't carry them in my pocket – I rarely had keys to the house in which I *did* live. In fact, I never went home unless I knew that someone would be waiting for me.

I told Kamil that I have a strange relationship with keys; that I've had no interest in keys for a long time. Since when? asked Kamil. Since the day I found a green notebook in a shop near our house, I told him. Its cover was made of fabric, embroidered with blue and red flowers. It also had a lock. I asked Baba for money to buy it and mentioned the lock. He firmly refused. He said there would be no secrets between us. He told me that we trusted each other, and that we were not afraid of being snooped on, because none of us went through each other's things. Our bedroom doors had no locks. In our family of three, our lives were open; no one was on their guard or felt embarrassed. The wooden dresser where I kept personal things had no locks on its drawers either, and my parents never looked in there because it was mine. So keys meant nothing to me. They became useless pieces of metal, and I could not stand to carry them or hear them clinking in my pocket or purse.

When I left Damascus in mid-June 2011, I did not take my house keys. Not because I did not think I would return, but because I was not accustomed to carrying them.

In the cold and gloomy Damascus International Airport, I sat on a metal chair with white enamel so scratched that only a few flecks remained. It was around three in the morning. I gazed at the duty-free shops selling Damascene sweets and supposedly traditional clothing. A sluggish cockroach with a heavy gait passed in front of me. It did not even stir fear in me. I wondered if Syrian cockroaches were suffering as well, if they too had lost all desire and moved lethargically now. I thought about running away from the airport and going home. But I remembered that I had checked in my bag. So what? My bag would travel on without me, then I would get it back in a few days. Eventually I decided against the idea. That was how things always went. I was sitting in the airport, thinking about going back, but I had lost my house for good. I no longer owned the thing to which I wanted to return. I had left my house in Damascus, and had no home to go back to. I may as well have been living in the airport, with all the planes taking me from homelessness to homelessness.

But . . . I did return to Damascus, a month and a half later. I stayed for two weeks. Then I went to Beirut on 12 August 2011. I left Damascus thinking that I would not stay in Lebanon more than a month or two. That was four and a half years ago.

I had expected Naseem to write about the revolution, but he couldn't seem to make progress in his novel without getting lost in the details. I remembered how we bickered about his inability to write. Naseem thought that current events were stalling his imagination. He said he could have written about a fictitious revolution, but that writing about the revolution happening in front of our eyes, something we had feelings about – that was too challenging. I thought that ignoring what was happening and writing about something unrelated was just a desperate attempt to escape reality. I was certain that the revolution had nothing to do with his inability to write from his imagination; I knew the real culprit was the medication he'd been taking daily since the revolution began, a final attempt at salvation. The antidepressants erased his imagination, along with his anxiety. He mocked me. 'It's just a little white tablet.'

Has he stopped taking medication in Germany? The

tablets he took with him must have run out by now, and he wouldn't get more without a prescription. Even as a general practitioner, Naseem can't write himself a prescription in Germany, and it would take effort, a little effort at least, to make an appointment with a psychiatrist. I understand Naseem well; I know him by heart. I know he won't make the effort. He won't have registered his medical degree or learned German so that he can practise medicine there.

(Was he even a real doctor, or a real writer? He was Naseem. He'd left his fear in the margins of his novel; had flirted with it, approaching yet never arriving.)

What revolution are you writing about, Naseem? The revolution ended the day you and everyone else left. Revolutions don't come from books, Naseem, they don't spring from words on the page. Revolution means begging my mother not to fall ill, every morning and night. My eyes silently plead for her to stay healthy, to not contract a virus or other disease. Do you know what happened to our neighbour Ferial? She fell ill. Got a bladder infection. Her son, who lives in France, told her, 'Don't worry about the money.' But medicine was expensive. They paid 70,000 lira for a bottle of antibiotics. Her condition didn't improve. The doctor suggested transferring her to the hospital, so they could give her a higher dosage intravenously. Meanwhile, her son called every day, and every day he said, 'Don't worry about the money.' But money wasn't the problem. Ferial needed to stay in the hospital for a week, but her daughter couldn't find a bed that would be available that long. She took a day off from work to search for one. Finding a hospital bed requires a vacation! Now that's revolution. She didn't even find half a bed, not even the right half where you feel you belong. Not even that. Her son sent money and they found a nurse instead, one who made daily house visits in exchange for a significant sum of cash, and she administered the serum for a week in their home. But Ferial didn't improve. Every time I visited their house, I heard her muttering: 'Oh Lord, let me rest. Take me, and let these children go home.' And so, silently I begged my own mother not to fall ill. I didn't have the strength to search for a hospital bed.

I wrote Naseem a letter but didn't send it. I added it to a stack of letters I hadn't sent. I described how Damascus had changed since he'd left. I told him I thought of him with every step I took outside the house. He would have found it difficult to handle life in this terrifying city. He would have been forced to face his fears every second. Traffic, cars packed bumper to bumper, waiting to proceed. Checkpoints, conscripts' questions. His fatal identity. Homs. Doctors leaving the country, hospitals unable to accept patients when people fell ill. You can't fall ill unexpectedly any more, or for free. You have to choose when your health will fail you, Naseem. Just the way you chose the moment of death for yourself, me, and your family. If you had stayed in Damascus, you would have killed yourself by now . . . well, maybe. Or maybe you would be losing yourself in wild parties, whose pulse reaches my ears on a constant, steady beat, honing the edge of my fear.

Kamil hasn't left Damascus yet, but he's exhausted just like us. We used to think him immune to exhaustion, frustration and depression, but he's not been his normal self. He greets me with a fraction of his usual energy, a sombre look and a practised smile.

I wonder how Kamil can treat *shabiha* and murderers. I've seen them in his waiting room, Naseem, on more than one occasion. Men with inflated muscles and broad shoulders, their expressions tinged with evil and fear. Have you ever seen evil coexist with fear? I've seen it in their eyes. They stare boldly, with impudence, at anyone, it doesn't matter who. How can Kamil accept their appointments? How can he listen to them? Do they tell him that they've killed? Do they speak of their pleasure in torturing people? Does one of them have Fouad's scent on his hands? Why do they come to see Kamil? Do they simply have an abundance of time and money? Or are they sent to confess how they abuse and torture others? Do they need practice at inventing insults to spit at whoever falls at their feet or into their grasp? I imagine rounds of torture all over again. I don't dare ask Kamil how he can accept appointments from men who stand at the edge of an abyss. How he can speak with perpetrators and victims alike. Does he treat them equally?

Neutrally, professionally? Does he help them build their self-confidence? Does he help them kill the way he helps us survive?

Could you bear sitting next to a man with bulked-up muscles in the waiting room where we first met? If your daydreaming gaze had wandered into his, where evil marches in stride with fear, would he have tolerated it?

I miss you and your anxious, ragged breath. I miss the scent of your sighs, to which I'm so attached. While you went on about what it means to belong somewhere, I never told you that the way your breath smells is one way I feel at home in my body; I belong to the blood that carries your body's scent through my veins.

Do you remember the last time I lay next to you? Do you remember how cautiously you kissed me, as if I were a stranger? Do you remember your obsession with people you imagined were watching us? Spying through your bedroom curtains, or from the light on the ceiling, or the cracks in your wardrobe with its contents so carefully arranged? Do you remember how many times you moved the huge desk in the living room, searching for a tiny camera fixed there? At the time, I didn't tell you that it was just fixed in your mind, something both simple and complex. I found no sign of it between the books. I never told you how often I wished I could find it and settle the matter. At one point I considered buying one and placing it between the books or hanging it from the curtains, before ripping it away, and ripping your fears away with it. But I abandoned the idea, because I thought this might also heighten your fears, make you more self-involved.

Hadn't we once agreed that as time goes by, life in this brutal city makes us believe we're important? Our egos swell, and we walk down the streets so full of ourselves. We all believe we're being followed, that we're an important target for the secret police. I didn't want to entrench this egotism further. But I did play along to ease your anxiety, and helped you put the desk back together, again and again. Do you remember that cautious kiss? It still pains me. Like a slap, it left a mark on my lips.

I see it in so many dreams. In one dream, I'm lying next to you. Gazing at your face, into your eyes. Contemplating your fear and anxiety, so pure that no comfort can touch them. I hear you ask me fearfully, 'Suleima, are you a frog?' I look at you. 'Of course not. If I'm a frog, does that make you a slice of orange?' I knew you hated the scent of oranges. I imagine you as a huge orange with a head on top. You sniff your orangey body, and then, like a parrot, repeat: 'I'm annoyed by how I smell, I'm annoyed by how I smell, I'm annoyed by how I smell.' I heard that sentence repeated in the dream, and when I woke up I couldn't tell whether you repeated it by yourself, or if I'd been chanting it with you, until for ever, endlessly.

Naseem's manuscript

As a child I often spent summer vacations in the village by myself, without my parents. Three months,
or a few days shy of that. The same thing happened
every time. The first day was the hardest. When
night fell, and the call to Isha' prayer rang out from
the mosque next to my grandfather's house, my
heart dressed itself in black. I missed my parents terribly, and begged my aunt to find a way to take me
back to Damascus. She always smiled and asked me
to be patient until morning, because she knew perfectly well that I would not raise the matter the next
day. She knew that before long, as days and then
weeks went by, I would count the nights left and cry
because time was passing so quickly.

I did call home every evening. In those days, phone
calls were difficult, incredibly complicated. There was
no direct line between Damascus and the other
governorates. First I called the telephone operator

(Central). I asked her to connect me to 423116 and hung up. The operator called them, and then routed the call back to me when she heard their phone ring. Meanwhile, I would be waiting by the phone for endless minutes, sometimes half an hour or a full hour, and if I called her back she'd snap: 'I'm trying, I'm trying . . . the line's busy.'

In the village, our choice of games was limited only by the number of streets, and the streets were endless. We left the house each morning and did not return until sundown. We roamed and explored shrines scattered around the village, where we always discovered puzzles and clues. Once we found verses from the Quran handwritten on a white slip of paper, and below them a note saying that whoever laid eyes on the verses must copy them one hundred times or be paralysed! My friends and I did not copy them, not even once. We decided to have a bit of fun.

We took the paper to Asia, a woman in her thirties whom my grandfather knew somehow. Asia: I imagined this was her name. She looked like an 'Asia', I could not say why. I never imagined another name for her. She was tall and slender, almost frighteningly so. Her skin was a translucent white; her soft, long hair was pitch-black, and always tied back with a green ribbon. Asia was incredibly impressionable and believed whatever she heard without stopping to consider whether or not it was true. She believed that if you left the house right after showering you would die. And that anyone who used scissors after sunset would be cursed with bad luck for life. If we told her we had seen a ghoul, she would have believed us and been frightened; she would shake so hard her joints would knock, and she'd refuse to leave the house for days.

We ran to her house from the shrine, and took a moment to tamp down our laughter as we caught our breath. We knocked on her door. She opened it and welcomed us in as usual. She was exceptionally generous, especially given how hard times had been for her. She opened the fridge and served us everything a child might wish for after a long day of playing and running around, oblivious to what we were hiding. We waited a few minutes, and then showed her the paper. She read it and gasped. She wished she had not read it. And then we left! Asia confined herself to the house until she had written the verse one hundred times, to save herself from paralysis. She never married; she's a spinster still. Maybe as a child she heard that marriage would kill her.

In the village, I was given freedom from every rule imaginable. This was in unspoken defiance of my mother. My family in the village believed she was too restrictive and probably prevented me from playing, going out in the street and mixing with other children. First off, she was neurotically clean, that's what they said in front of me, bluntly and often: 'Really obsessive.' On top of that, she was a Damascus, big-city girl: playing in the street didn't feature in her idea of childhood. Of course, as a child she had spent whole days playing on the block. 'It was different back then . . .' they said, taking sides, and of course there was some truth to that.

I could put on a white dress and spend the whole day playing, and it would remain spotless all day! I always gave a wide berth to anything that would make it dirty. I remember people in the village trading jokes about my soap-swallowing addiction too. Between seven and nine years old, I was addicted to eating soapsuds: I would wash my hands well, foam up the soap, and then, with ravenous desire, bite into the bubbles. They said my mother's neuroticism must have tricked me into thinking that soap would disinfect my insides!

My mother once came to the village on an unexpected visit. It had been more than a month since I had arrived, enough time for me to become a different child. I remember her silence. I was wearing red nail polish, and my fringe was coiffed with hairpins like a rooster's comb (years later, this would be in vogue) and stuck straight up, cliff-like, atop my forehead. I was using words she had never heard, liberated from every restriction and obligation, thoroughly debauched. She said nothing, but her look alone was enough to make my fringe collapse. She took me back with her to Damascus, and back to what was, in her opinion, right.

My mother says that when I was six or seven, she took me to a friend's jewellery shop to buy a present for another friend who had just given birth to her first child. I was wearing a burgundy velvet dress, and a hat in the same colour. When I sat on a tall chair that was burgundy too, the jeweller looked over and said, 'Ah, bless! Your girl's a little princess, isn't she.' They were engrossed in the bracelets and rings on display when suddenly they heard a soft voice say, 'Mama, can I have some water?' Recently back from summer in the village, I had asked in an Alawite dialect. My mother said the shopkeeper was stunned and looked around for the source of the voice, in disbelief that it could have been me.

The accent signalled a history's worth of stereotypes and the suffering of millions; dialect alone was enough to unleash its savagery. The anecdote was notable because it was so dark. The accent was a stark contrast to my burgundy dress and title of 'princess'. It didn't fit boys and girls of the big city, who were so refined their ancestors must have heralded from palaces, not far-flung and half-forgotten coastal villages. Anyone who spoke with an Alawite accent was assumed to be a country bumpkin, and anyone who spoke with a Damascus (or 'neutral') accent was clearly an urbanite. This wasn't just about a burgundy dress worn by a 'princess sitting on a burgundy throne'. The associations it conjured were as intricate as the stitching of the dress itself.

You only needed to say that someone had 'an accent' for anyone to understand the implication: it was Alawite. It was the only accent that had this much power, capable of transforming a simple, downtrodden man into a swaggering force, someone who could saunter into the middle of Damascus and defy the authority of traffic officers, government officials, pedestrians, street vendors, and anyone who fell short of perfection. Accent was identity. And not just any identity; the identity of absolute power, an identity shared by the dictator and tyrant. The identity of terror, anonymity and dread. Anyone who spoke it perfectly found that shortcuts and loopholes magically appeared; it was invaluable to getting by in a country like Assad's Syria.

The accent's power had distilled with time. Eventually, you did not need to speak in a full Alawite accent to wield its effects. Even just properly pronouncing your T's was enough to spark terror and summon a history of oppression in an instant, the brief instant it took to pronounce a T. Slurs like 'dogs', 'rats' and 'vermin' were practically the extent of certain sects' vocabulary.

I still do not know the origins of certain odd words in the Alawite accent. Some come from Turkish or Ottoman, like *khashouqa*, which means 'spoon', but other expressions have roots that are harder to trace.

For example, one time many years ago, a relative of mine, an architectural engineer who rarely visited the village, asked his grandmother – who was my great-aunt, grandmother Khadija's sister – 'Sitti, why d'you call Baba "Jakjouk?" ' Jakjouk, a derivation of Jack-in-the-box, was his father's nickname in the village. What did his grandmother say? *'Zee wurna cree.'* My friend was bewildered; he had not understood a single word. Making sense of her reply was harder than filling a sieve with water. He tried to decipher each word separately. (*Zee*: 'because he'; *wurna*: 'was in a'; *cree*: 'scurry' or 'rush' or 'hurry'.) When my cousin wanted to show how much she liked something, she would say: '*Aman*, how lovely!' *Aman* comes from Turkish, too. When expressing surprise, her favourite phrase was 'Oh myyyyyyyyy,' and she always let the 'Y' extend until infinity, stretching it until her breath ran out, like a deep-sea diver. When she made fun of other people for putting on airs – a poor man acting as if he would become rich overnight, or a young woman of average beauty acting as if all the young village men were courting her – then came the phrase 'Oh Lord', but the vowels grew rounder in her mouth, so the

O's became U's: 'Uh Lurd.' Negation didn't exist in dialect. For example, instead of saying 'can't', people from the village said 'cann', extending the penultimate consonant instead of pronouncing the T. 'Won't' became 'wonn', 'didn't' became 'dinn', and so on. As for final consonants, people in the village tended to trail off at the end of their words. 'Home' became 'ho . . . ': the sound of the H and O remained, while the M and E gently faded away. A friend used to tease us, saying, 'You goin' ho . . . to eat hu . . . ?' The subtle shift in vowel – from O to U – was all that distinguished 'home' and 'hummus' in his question.

Another thing I never understood was a tendency towards using classical Arabic when speaking to important people (public figures). No sooner does an Alawite sit down with an important figure than he puts on an air of erudition, and tries hard to employ a higher register. I remember my father's cousin, a low-ranking officer in the army, who once called my mother and I while we were out. It was a few months after Baba passed away, and Abu Jamil wanted to check in on us. The phone rang several times before the answering machine picked up. He figured that an answering machine requires the same formality as a letter, and so he left us the following message, word for word: 'Dearest ones, I hereby have called, yet found an empty abode. As it was my wish to enquire after you, I might request that you return my message when convenient. Sincerely, Abu Jamil.'

I also remember a joke about an officer who only wanted to receive Alawite visitors. He told a conscript to place a bottle of water on the table in the entryway and ask each guest: 'What is this?' If the guest answered 'A jug of water' and properly pronounced the T, the conscript allowed him in to see the officer. But if the guest swallowed his T's and said 'A jug of wa'er,' the conscript would tell him the officer was busy and show him the door. One day, the conscript rushed into the officer's office and said, 'Sir, there's a man says it's a carafe, I donn know wha' to do, should I lettim in?' The officer laughed delightedly. 'Show him in, show him in,' he said. 'He's clearly more cultured than either of us!'

Dialect was not the only thing shaped by sectarianism; certain sheikhs in these villages possessed 'divine abilities'. I remember one summer vacation, when my grandmother thought a patch of spots (eczema) near my elbow looked suspicious. All she did was send me to her sister's husband (the architectural engineer's grandfather), a prominent sheikh in the village. He said he would write a charm for me to wear underneath my clothes like an amulet, and the spots would disappear. I went to see him with my youngest cousin, the one with the booming voice that always forced my aunt to acquiesce. We entered his room by the little vegetable patch, near the house where his son's family lived. He was eating lunch and his mouth was filled with bits of food. I showed him my rash. And what did he do? He spat on a scrap of fabric and rubbed my arm with his saliva and bits of food. Then he wrote a charm for me and told me to put it under my pillow. Needless to say, my eczema did not disappear until my mother took me to a dermatologist in Damascus.

My father did not leave me a family when he passed away. He was my family, all of it, and then he was gone. He left me his mother and childhood home, and his books, papers, journals, photographs and pens.

And what did Naseem leave me, aside from books, papers, journals, photographs and pens? He left me obituaries too, and a home that didn't look like the one where we'd spent years together. My mother never asks me about him. Just like she never asks about Fouad. Maybe she assumes that in war it's men's duty to disappear, whether on the battlefront, in prison or in exile. She never asks about the men we've known for so long. Only about the women. My mother, how strange she is! If my father were still alive, I'm sure she would have separated from him. He wouldn't have enlisted at his age, and might not have taken a clear position on the war. She wouldn't have been able to abide staying with a man who chose to hide instead of disappearing.

My mother, who has lost her only son, seems proud for the first time in her life, proud that her lost son has given her life meaning again. Fouad has given her the ability to keep on going, for days or even weeks, between the covers of a book, on page 24. Naseem, however, I don't think she ever liked. She saw a miniature copy of her husband in him: a doctor, a man who abandoned his family and fled in fear. Naseem was also afraid of fear, so he summoned it and let it overwhelm him. In the end, the result was the same.

I remember the day, before Fouad disappeared, before Naseem left for Germany, when Naseem showed up unexpectedly around lunchtime. He knocked loudly, as forcefully as someone who had arrived to pick a fight or murder or assassinate someone, and that was the best-case scenario. I ran to the door. My mother was unaffected by any noise outside the gloomy spot in her memory that she inhabited at that time. I was surprised. She seemed isolated, her feelings undisturbed by external factors like a sharp knock at the door, the telephone ringing in the middle of the night, or even the sound of an explosion. (She isn't affected or struck with panic like I am, even though she is entitled to be afraid. She carries thirty more years of memories than I do.)

That afternoon, I ran to the door while she sat in front of her bowl of lentil soup, eating at her own pace, as if all of time would unfurl itself while she finished her lunch. I opened the door and found Naseem. He could barely stand. He was panting, and sweat poured down his forehead and all over his body, leaving dark patches under his armpits, tracing the folds of his stomach and running down his back. He told me he was dying. My mother remained sitting at her bowl, showing no sign of interest.

I led him to the living room and helped him lie down on the sofa. I brought him a bag of ice and put it on his forehead, just like he told me to. With that, he regained his medical abilities, and began dictating to me what else I should do in a moment like this. The sharp cold would slow his racing heart, he said. He closed his eyes, and words tumbled from his mouth. He said he was dying and he was afraid and he didn't want to die now because he wasn't ready.

I asked if a person could ever truly be ready for death. Were the stories told at funerals true? At every memorial service I'd been to, I'd heard relatives of the deceased say things like, 'For the first time in his life, he said goodbye when he left the house that day, as if he knew it would be the last time.' (Usually the people who told these stories were young, not middle-aged. Older people don't feel death immediately at hand so much as sense it drawing closer, every moment, every day, until it arrives.) Or relatives would say that before passing away, the soon-to-be deceased began speaking to people no one else could see. Those people were never from the world of the living, naturally; they might be a long-dead mother, a father who had passed away several years earlier, or a friend who had died young. The ailing man would begin speaking to them as if they had just entered the room, called his name and asked him to join them in travelling from our world to theirs. These were depressing stories, and made death seem all the more depressing too.

On the sofa, Naseem kept saying he wasn't ready to die. What did it mean to be ready to die? How could one be prepared for death? He got up and rushed through all the rooms of the house. He said he was looking for something. Maybe he was looking for his soul, maybe it had fled his body in fear, gasping for air in a body undergoing a panic attack. Like a madman he ran from my mother's bedroom to my bedroom, to Fouad's room, to the toilet. He turned on the tap and put his head under the rush of water, and said it wasn't cold enough to breathe! Could he breathe underwater like a fish? He dried his face, went back to the living room and lay down on the long sofa again. I followed him into the room. He picked up the bag of ice he'd tossed on the wooden coffee table and put it on his head, then pressed it to his forehead, then his cheeks. That wasn't enough, so he opened the bag and took out a piece of ice. He ran it over his stomach. It melted with the heat of his body, and the water dripped onto the red sofa and made dark spots on the fabric. Naseem was drowning in sweat, ice melt, and fear. His fear rose steadily until it reached its zenith, and then began to drop, incrementally, degree by degree. He told me that fear struck him all at once, rushing through his veins (Naseem frequently used vaguely medical metaphors). And when it faded, it did so excruciatingly slowly; it took an exhausting amount of time.

Naseem eventually calmed down. My mother was still sitting in front of her bowl of lentil soup, eating steadily, as if nothing were amiss. She entered the living room after she'd finished her food, and after he'd calmed down, after his soul had returned to his tired body. She sat down across from him, and looked into his eyes. 'Have you eaten lunch, Naseem?' she asked softly. He didn't answer. He apologised for his sudden visit, thanked me for my concern, and left. The door had barely closed behind him when she uttered her favourite phrase: 'Poor Naseem.'

Was Naseem Dr Soufjan from Shami Hospital? I wondered as I thought about his book. I knew Naseem had worked in that hospital. He complained of encountering death every day in the corridors, hospital beds and operating rooms. He told me that death had a certain scent. He often smelled it while examining a patient who had just departed from this world. He once told me about a cancer patient who spent a month in the hospital before he died, with his wife by his side. A few minutes before midnight, his wife left the room and came to the counter where the on-duty doctors and nurses sat, and asked Naseem to come with her to her husband's room. He went in and saw that the patient's eyes were closed. 'Is he gone?' she asked. (I remember the word as if he said it today: 'gone'.) Naseem examined him and realised there was still a slow, weak pulse in his veins. Naseem shook his head. The wife was a few moments too early. She whispered in her husband's ear, words Naseem couldn't catch. Her husband opened his eyes and managed a smile. Then he then let out a brief exhalation and closed his eyes again. The woman looked at Naseem, and asked him to examine her husband again. Naseem approached and caught that strange scent, the whiff of death. He knew her husband was 'gone' without feeling for a pulse. He placed the stethoscope on the man's chest, and could hear that his heartbeat had stopped. Complete silence. Her husband was gone.

Naseem, a man who feared water, told me that in his mind, death was like the moment you plunge into the sea, when all external sound disappears and only a deep internal sound remains. It was silence. Deep silence, undisturbed by anything. But Naseem never mentioned that this patient had a daughter who was, and still is, fourteen.

Naseem's manuscript

My mother sat in the waiting room with a friend of the family, smoking silently. My father's room was down the hallway. The waiting room was not sectioned off from the corridor or other hospital rooms by a door, and smoking was permitted at the time. Suddenly my mother broke the silence, handed the friend her cigarette, and excused herself. She gave him the cigarette because she thought she would only be gone for a moment.

Later, my mother told me that she had heard a deep voice calling her name. She immediately knew that it was her husband. He called to her without parting his lips, not even slightly. She went into his room, which was filled with friends standing around his bed. As she approached him, they stepped back and moved to the foot of his bed. She sat on the edge of the bed and stroked his head. He opened his eyes, with effort, and looked at her. She bent down and whispered in his right ear: 'You can go, *habibi*. I'm with you . . . you can go, sweetheart.' He smiled at her and closed his eyes. My mother looked at Soufjan. 'Is that it?' she asked. 'Is he gone?'

Soufjan approached, checked my father's wrist for a pulse, and found it. He shook his head. She drew close to him again. She whispered in the same ear, 'It's OK, *habibi* . . . darling, go on . . . I'm here with you.' He gazed at her deeply, as if his eyes were fixing themselves to hers for eternity. As if he were giving her his radiance before it was extinguished, pouring it into her eyes so she could carry it with her for the rest of her life. Then he briefly frowned, let out a deep exhalation, and was gone. Yes. My father didn't pass until his wife told him he could go. Years earlier they had agreed that she would help him when the time came. They renewed their pact frequently, as if it were the air my father needed to breathe. Once his wife told him it was OK to go, he knew that passing was the only way, and he did not linger.

Someone who writes things like this isn't mad. But for years my mother has insisted that Naseem has lost his mind, just as she insists that she's losing her memory. She hasn't forgotten the time he arrived at our house at one o'clock in the morning. He woke us all up: my mother, Fouad and me. My mother, as usual, was not unnerved to hear the doorbell ring after midnight, but Fouad and I rushed to the door. We opened it to find Naseem standing there, his face damp and pale with fear. He asked if he could spend the night. He said he'd been lying in bed when he heard strange noises outside the door. He'd quietly got up and looked through the peephole. He didn't see anyone, but he felt like a person, or people, had been there and left. He'd dressed quickly, cautiously opened the front door and gone down a flight of stairs to the ground floor. He ran through the streets until he found a taxi and came to our house. With conviction, he said they were still following him. 'Who's "they"?' my mother asked. Naseem didn't know, not exactly. But he was sure they were watching and following him.

'Poor Naseem. He went mad,' my mother still says, as matter-of-factly as someone commenting that the weather is cold.

In our house that night, Naseem remembered that amid all the chaos and unnerving details, he'd glimpsed a black bag of garbage stacked by his front door. This surprised him. It must be a message that they wanted him to decipher, he said. I told Naseem that my father, too, was always afraid that 'they' were suspicious of him – despite the portrait hanging in his office, and despite his complicit silence, for which my mother never forgave him. Who were 'they'? I didn't know, we didn't know, and my father didn't know. Naseem also claimed 'they' were following him, spying on his movements, monitoring his every breath. They were watching him in his bed, on the right half; they held in their grip the one place he belonged.

'So what if they don't believe me?' my father often said. What more could he do, beyond running away to Damascus and 'treating the people who lived there instead of his own kin in Hama,' as my mother said he had done? What more could he control, beyond hanging a portrait in his office, high on the wall above everything else? What more could I do to allay his fears, beyond participating in Young Revolutionaries and Pioneers concerts at school, using my bold voice to sing 'Oh Abu

Bassel, our Leader with the high forehead' and 'O Syria, through you I'm free! You gave to me my dignity.' Yes, I lent my voice to these songs for years, singing of dignity and freedom at the top of my lungs without ever considering what the words meant.

Was that not enough for you, Baba? Didn't I excuse you from the obvious questions about dignity, freedom and occupied lands? About National Education lessons and principles of war? About our teacher at school who disappeared after her five-year-old son let the President's picture trail on the ground behind him? We were celebrating the 'Corrective Movement', which began with a coup led by Hafez al-Assad. Nationalist songs filled the courtyard and made their way to surrounding homes that day, Syrian and Ba'ath Party flags fluttered everywhere, and pictures of the eternal leader covered the walls. They had been hastily affixed, though, with shiny silver duct tape. All her five-year-old son did was tear one down and drag it along behind him, on the ground. The teacher disappeared from school after that, and we heard she was disappeared for good.

This story aside, didn't I tolerate your anxiety, Baba? Did you know that when I was in Year 10, the youth military-education instructor asked me into her office. It looked much like yours. 'Suleima, your family is from Hama,' she began. 'Has your father told you what happened there?' No sooner had her question slithered into my ears than I transformed into you. I saw you entering my body, your eyes filling mine. I was you. Immediately my stomach cramped, the way yours would have done if you had been there. I won't forget how weak my knees became, how fragile I felt, oh Baba. My inconsequential life was reduced to the vibrations of her voice. 'Our Father the Leader has bloodied his hands for the entire Syrian people,' I replied. I waited for her response: a frown, or a contented smile. She smiled and told me I was free to go. I desperately wanted her to do something – shout at me, for instance; slap, kick or report me to the Wise Leadership, with orders to assassinate you and Mother! Or for her to have said: 'Bravo! Your family raised you well.' Instead, her cryptic smile kept me up night after night, imagining what might be in store. Here, I'm speaking again about fear of fear. Anticipating fear is harder than feeling it. Prison is easier than fearing it. Fear on its own is less cruel than fearing fear.

Has Naseem really lost his mind?

Naseem's manuscript

Yasmine called me one morning from a Lebanese phone number, and said she was in Beirut for the week. More than a year had passed since her family had all seen each other, so they had decided to meet in Beirut. She arrived from Damascus with her mother, father and brother. Her older sister flew in from Dubai with her husband and children. And her younger sister travelled from Germany with her husband. They came to spend New Year's Eve together in a cheap hotel halfway down Hamra Street, and planned to return to their respective homes on New Year's Day. I hadn't seen them since the revolution began.

I had not forgotten the years we all lived on the first floor of a building in Masaken Barzeh. The girls were open and friendly, and we all grew up together. I had been completely alone in those days, and they were like sisters to me. Then came the rift. It happened quietly, no shouting, confessions or discussion.

They stopped calling, and I knew. It was not hard to understand. Things were not the way they had been before the revolution. The rift was self-evident, and there was no need to try to repair it or restore what used to be.

But now she had called and reached out, and I was happy to hear from her after so many years. I went to the hotel to see them. They had two small adjacent rooms shared by the whole family. Even for someone who had never met them before and did not know them at all, it would not have been hard to tell who had come from Damascus and who lived abroad, free from the madness that Syrian cities had become. My friend's body appeared feeble and slack, and the same was true for her mother, father and brother. Her sisters coming from Dubai and Germany looked robust, though, with a blush of contentment on their cheeks.

Those coming from Damascus politely declined to meet in public, explaining that they were a bit unsettled and did not feel like going out to a coffee shop. I understood. It was not hard to understand. Things were not the way they had been before the revolution. We sat together in their hotel room and made a real effort to avoid discussing politics. This proved difficult if one considered power blackouts, rising prices, shelling, mortars, checkpoints and fear to be political. But they saw nothing 'political' about any of this; in their eyes it could all be explained by conspiracy theories. Then, even though they had refused to meet in public because they would 'rather not go out', they left the hotel, all except for Yasmine. She was tense, and it became clear that she wanted them to leave so she could be alone with me. I returned my cup of coffee to the room's kitchenette. I didn't tell her that I avoid coffee in the evening. I had a strange feeling that saying anything about my habits, preferences or even my mood would be excessive.

We each lit a cigarette. Conversation was slow at first, as if we had just met, as if the river of our shared memories had run dry when the revolution began in 2011. I asked her how work was going and she responded briefly, though not discourteously. 'It's going. We're getting by, thankfully.'

Slowly, we opened up to each other again. Yasmine told me that her salary was less than two hundred dollars a month, and that she spent most of that on public transportation between her home in Masaken Barzeh and her job in Firdous. What remained was not enough to buy a cup of coffee in a café, she said, much less clothes or other necessities. She told me that by last month she had managed to save five thousand lira, which used to be worth a hundred dollars. But now it barely amounted to ten. The airline company where she had worked for more than a year now required her to wear a skirt as part of its uniform, and she had wanted to buy wool tights to wear underneath . . . but they cost three thousand lira! All day she booked tickets from Damascus to Dubai or Egypt for passengers who were turning to private companies now that the national airline's fleet has been reduced to a single plane. She said that she held passports, airline tickets and hotel reservations in her hands every day, but never dreamed of leaving that dreary swamp herself.

In an effort to make the conversation more natural, like it used to be, I asked her if she still cried. Before the revolution, Yasmine used to come over with a little bag and spend days or weeks at our house. She said she felt like a stranger in her home. I never understood where her sense of alienation came from: she was so similar to them, as they were to us. But she was constantly lonely, as if her soul had been born into the wrong skin, as if she belonged to her family and home in body alone. She often lived with us for long periods, and we would almost forget she was there. The only reminder was the sound of her crying emanating from the little room where she slept, the one that used to be mine. She cried feverishly, without a clear sense of why. Maybe she needed a daily cry to wash away some obscure pain.

Sitting there years later with our cigarettes, I asked her if she still cried. She gave me her old, sweet smile . . . and began to cry. Had I reminded her of her tears? I don't know. She cried and cried. I smiled tenderly, and encouraged her to talk to me.

She said she was deeply in love with a young man named Mahdi. She had met him at the checkpoint erected in front of her grandmother's house in Damascus, in the neighbourhood of Mazraa. Yasmine stopped to check in on her grandmother every evening on her way home from work. The taxi stopped at the checkpoint, and each time the man asked for her ID and smiled at her. Yasmine fell in love faster than you could write the word, and they started meeting at his house in Mezzeh. She was so in love! I felt a lump in my throat when she told me about Mahdi. She said that he had texted her a few minutes ago to tell her that a decision had been made to transfer him to Harasta, to fight on the side of the regime's army. 'I don't know if I'll see him again,' she said through tears. 'What if he dies?'

I suddenly felt light-headed and unable to breathe. Panic gripped my lungs and squeezed my chest. I took a whole Xanax. She said his family refused to let them marry because she was Sunni and he was Shiite. My fingers began to tremble and I lost the ability to speak. I could not even maintain a kind, empathetic gaze to soothe her. Could I offer consolation for her boyfriend being transferred to the Harasta battlefront? Harasta, where my uncle lived before the revolution began, from where he was forced to flee when the regime's army bombed and invaded the city, where houses were destroyed and lives stolen. How could I console her, when her lover was going to fight against civilians in retreat? I asked her how she could love a killer. This surprised her. She said that he joined the combat so as not to be killed. I hope he *does* get killed, I said to myself, and then repeated the phrase, repeated it until it echoed in my mind, until I could no longer distinguish its reverberation from her words or the cars passing under the window.

Cutting her off mid-sentence, I stood abruptly, went to the window, opened it, stuck my head out, and inhaled the damp, chilly air. It had started to drizzle. I felt as though I couldn't breathe. I went to the sofa, where I had haphazardly tossed my things. A packet of cigarettes; my purse, scarf and coat. Suddenly I felt as if these scattered things were my soul, or a collection of memories. And then a sense of being lost, estranged, and separate from reality swept over me again. I felt so heavy and so light at the same time! My head was empty all of a sudden, yet I struggled to keep it on my shoulders; it felt detached from my body, and I was filled with a sense of absence. My soul was in my eyes alone; they were my window to the outside world, as I felt my way along my numb body to be sure it was really there.

Yasmine was crying and talking about Mahdi, and meanwhile I was suffocating. I interrupted her. I told her the story of the underwear. I don't know why her talk of Mahdi reminded me of it; I had heard it a year earlier, and it had stayed with me. It was the story of an officer in the army who was suspected of being a potential deserter and detained. He was stripped of all his clothes, even his underwear, and left naked. Then he was thrown into a small room with other naked men. Only one among them was wearing underwear, and though they were tattered, he was the envy of everyone else. Why were they all naked, they wondered, while this man's genitals were covered? Why *him*? Every morning, the men were led in procession for a short round of torture, the first of a long day that would see many more.

One morning the man with the underwear was brought back to the room and its stench of hot breath, pus and disease. He was thrown to the floor, tortured so severely that he collapsed. He was bleeding everywhere and his eyes shone with pain. He groaned, his vacant gaze roving across the room, until finally he closed his eyes and passed away. The rest of the men fought and wrestled, swearing at each other, using the last of their strength to win the underwear. But it was the officer who emerged victorious and put it on. Only then did they realise the story behind it: it was a trophy to be won by a single man, who would not relinquish it until he died or was released.

Yasmine fell silent, and I made an excuse to leave. I walked through the streets of Hamra in the light rain, searching for air and some sense of security. No, we could never live together again. That was what I was thinking.

Has Naseem lost his mind? Did he lose it in Damascus, or under the rubble of their house in Homs, or in Germany? Or did he lose it in the 'Department of Death and Madness', where he was held for thirty days? Naseem wasn't involved in the protests, and hadn't participated in any suspicious gatherings. But he had come to our house often, and had a good relationship with Fouad.

One morning about three months before Fouad disappeared, Naseem went out and was detained. They thought he was coming over to meet with my brother. When they found out he was a doctor, and from Homs, their suspicions grew. They dragged him to Department 215, or the 'Department of Death and Madness', as it was known. Naseem spent thirty days in a four-by-five-metre cell with more than ninety other detainees. They were packed in so tight he couldn't even raise his arms. A single mass of bodies, all the arms as if amputated: one body with more than ninety heads. Naseem told me that there were ninety-nine of them, and that each head bore one of the ninety-nine names of God. There was al-Jabbar, al-Mo'men, al-Shaheed, al-Hayy, al-Haq, al-Haleem and al-Sabbour . . . names meaning the Almighty, the Guardian of Faith, the Witness, the Immortal, the Truth Embodied, the Patient One . . . My mother couldn't hold her tongue when she heard this, and whispered in my ear, 'So which one was Naseem? The All-Hearing? The Watchful One?'

Naseem said that one day the head next to him took his hand, leaned in close and whispered, 'You know . . . this place isn't that bad. We're starting to really love it here.' These words sent a shiver through Naseem's soul – Naseem, who considered love to be nothing more than habit! Would they be detained long enough to grow accustomed to this place, and come to love it? Who was it who said this – was it 'the All-Seeing' or 'the All-Knowing'?

Naseem was never beaten. Even so, he wished for death every moment of those thirty days, he said. It was over 50 degrees Celsius in the 'dormitory', as the cell was called, and the air was thick with the prisoners' breathing. Exhalations accumulated in impenetrable layers, and it was hard to find a fresh gulp of air in between. Bodies deteriorated quickly, overtaken by rashes, scabies and pus-filled sores. People went mad in there. They beat each other in a fight for survival. Prisoners hit each other, aiming to kill, just for an extra sip of oxygen, a body's width of space, or room to raise their hand even slightly. They barely ate or drank. Emaciated: that was the word that described them all. Prominent bones. Skin hanging in folds, or stretched concave over empty bodies. Bulging eyes sunken into sockets. Everyone crammed against each other, everyone's limbs sticking out of everyone else. You might see a prisoner's foot protruding from someone else's mouth. One person's head sprouting from another's stomach. Like an insane asylum. Everyone wanted to kill everyone else. Everyone lost consciousness at times, or entered a tunnel of hallucination and scrabbled for something that would never be found. Some survived. Many did not.

After thirty days in the Department of Death and Madness, Naseem was taken to Department 227. There, 'conditions improved': only twenty detainees in a seven-by-twelve-metre room. They tortured him twice, beating him with a metal pipe that had turned green with corrosion, an 'Abrahamic green', as the other prisoners said. Prisoners were beaten on their bruises. Naseem tried to kill himself by scratching at his body and ripping his limbs apart. He tried to strip his skin from his soul. But his soul fought back . . . and madness was how it resisted.

Fouad was crushed by what happened to Naseem, and held himself responsible. My mother made light of it, saying Fate clearly wanted Naseem to be detained; the experience would make him a bit braver, and breathe life into his clearly ailing conscience in his prison of a soul. After all, his family was dying in the siege of Homs. I didn't argue with her about his conscience.

When given an opportunity, my mother could never hold her tongue. She had lost her brother in the Hama massacre more than three decades earlier, but had never lost hope of his return. I often imagined his homecoming. He had been fifty at the time, so, if he really was alive, he'd be nearer ninety by now.

Has Naseem lost his mind? I sat in Kamil's waiting room, so packed it had begun to feel more and more like a hospital. Instead of extending hours for appointments, Kamil had reduced them under the pretext of the security situation; he said he wanted to be sure that his commute home to Bab Touma and Leila's commute to Masaken Barzeh were safe. Prior to the revolution, he always took Fridays and Sundays off, but now he closed the office on Saturdays too.

Sitting in the small waiting room wasn't as nice as it used to be. After Naseem left, it felt constricting, and I often thought I heard his footfall coming up or down the stairs. I remembered the chair where he sat, as if he belonged there. I remembered his wandering gaze, how he lost himself in thought, and the smoke of his cigarette when he ashed it. He would look directly at Leila every time, as if he were doing her a favour by using the ashtray.

On Kamil's face I saw lines etched by exhaustion. It

occurred to me that for the first time in his life he was experiencing the same thing we were: we the crushed, unnerved and frightened ones. We were all feeling the same thing, and he was one of us now. He suffered as we do, living in fear of checkpoints, attacks, shelling and death.

The time before, I had asked him if madness had a clear starting point. Did it begin gradually, or did it happen all at once? What makes a person lose their mind?

Kamil gave a brief smile, then quickly focused his attention. 'Are you afraid you're going mad?'

For a moment I was silent. 'Yes,' I blurted out. 'I'm afraid of going crazy the way my mum became an old woman – overnight.'

He laughed, exhaled a puff of smoke and shook his head with a slightly exaggerated gesture. 'Don't worry . . . you won't go mad until we all do.'

His response confused me. Before the revolution, Kamil had never spoken about 'us' as an entity. He talked to me about myself, distinct from anyone else. One time I wanted to give him a painting I'd done, though finishing it had given me a panic attack, and told him it might help him understand the intensity of fear that moved in my mind. But Kamil had refused the gift, insisting on maintaining a professional relationship between himself and his clients.

That was the incredibly thin but intentional line Kamil had guarded, no different from other doctors and therapists. The revolution had snapped that line. Irreparably. We weren't standing on opposite banks any more, we stood on the same shore; even *shabiha* still coming to see him had joined our ranks. Apparently Kamil believed that either we all stood together or we'd all lose our minds at once! Did we all possess the same degree of strength? Was Kamil so overwhelmed that he thought the current situation was stronger than all of us, more than we could bear, more powerful than each of us individually? Is that how we became *all of us*, not *each of us*?

I told him that in my dream I'd been in my father's clinic in the Italian quarter. I didn't know how I got in. His office was on the first floor of an old building with high ceilings in the Ain al-Kirish neighbourhood. There was a little room upstairs with a window-sized door; I'd somehow got in and had sat down by the door. Naseem was standing on the ground below, looking up at me. I was in his clinic. He wasn't wearing a white coat. He was in jeans and a light green cotton jumper. He stood there, cocked his head and gently said, 'Come on, now . . . come on down, *habibti.*' I was surprised to hear him say *habibti*; rarely did he call me 'darling'. I refused. I wanted to keep hiding there, though I didn't know what I was hiding from. Kamil smiled. He said matter-of-factly, as if the dream were a cliché: 'You miss your father, and you replaced him with Naseem.'

Naseem's manuscript

I did not know it would be my last visit to Damascus. I left Beirut at three in the afternoon. For the previous few months I had preferred having Hassan drive me instead of Mohammed; even though I had known Mohammed for years, his needling questions about current events made me nervous. It was never casual curiosity or commiseration; his questions felt more intimate and had a whiff of the secret police.

'Do we have a choice, aside from Bashar?' he said once. 'I mean, don't get me wrong here . . . but we could probably do better, don't you think?' This he said emphatically, and then leaned forward slightly to look me in the eye in the rear-view mirror. I was silent.

Hassan was in his fifties, and more genuine than Mohammed. He talked about what was happening in the country too, but never concealed anything behind his words, no matter how harsh they might be.

We left Beirut at three in the afternoon, and by quarter to four we'd gone no further than Hazmieh, on the outskirts of the city, less than six kilometres away. It was Friday and the traffic was at its peak.

'Did you hear what happened to Mohammed?' asked Hassan. He continued without waiting for me to respond. 'May he rest in peace. He was coming back from Jdeidet Artouz a week ago. He owed money to a man, a member of the *shabiha*, and hadn't yet paid . . . They killed him in front of his kids, right there in the car.'

I felt sorry when I heard this. Though I had known that Mohammed was working with the *mukhabarat*, I also knew how hard times had been for his family. He had three boys and four girls, and no one in the family had finished school. How could anyone survive amid news of death and murder every day? Did some of us deserve death and others not? Would I have felt worse if Hassan had been the one killed? Had the revolution turned us into people who doled out death or remorse according to victims' deeds? Had this brutal regime turned us into brutes ourselves, brutes who choose who should be killed?

We reached the Lebanese border, crossed the no-man's-land and arrived at the Syrian side. The traffic was unbearable. The lists of wanted people, formerly maintained by the Immigration and Passports Office, were now held at the border checkpoint.

Several junior and senior officers were stationed there, all with the same disinterested expression, and most of them had a cigarette stuck between drooping lips. Aggravation. More aggravation. Even when they detained you, they did so with just a degree of irritation, as if detaining people was a daily occurrence, no stranger than the common cold.

The officer inspected my passport closely. He said my name then, loudly, as if he wanted me to respond, to identify myself among the other passengers. But the only other person in the car was Hassan; did he think Hassan would respond when he shouted my name?

He said my name again, my full name. Then he took my passport and went into the cement building – one room only, clearly hastily constructed – to an officer sitting behind an ancient little computer. I could see him speaking to the other officer and giving him my passport. Then they signalled me over. Hassan said apprehensively that if the unthinkable happened, he would continue on to Damascus and tell my mother that I had been detained.

I got out of the car, feeling incredibly anxious. I walked to the building and went in. The officer sitting behind the computer stared at me with contempt. He shook his head, and the cigarette dangling between his lips shook too.

'Where's your father?' he asked.

I smiled, in an attempt to show my confusion. 'Baba? He's been gone for a long time now,' I said.

He let out a sneering laugh. 'Where'd he go? Fled with the rest of the traitors?'

'He's dead,' I said, and thought of Kamil. The officer raised an eyebrow in surprise. He asked me for my father's date of death, and his surprise grew when I said he'd passed away more than fifteen years ago. He looked at his computer, then back at my passport.

'Why are you asking about Baba?' I ventured.

He replied with a degree of annoyance that was clearly constant. 'Your father's a wanted man. We need to know where he is.'

I told him there must be someone else with the same name. He raised his eyebrows again, this time to tell me I was wrong. 'Your father's a writer, isn't he?' I nodded. 'Yeah, he's a wanted man,' he confirmed.

He gave me my passport, and I left. Are they trying to detain the dead now, too?

When I finally arrived, at seven at night, my mother was waiting for me. I told her that they wanted to arrest her husband, and that she needed to stay alert. Then, somehow, this sentence emerged from my lips: 'On the border today, just a little while ago, actually – Baba died.'

I wandered through the house, as I did every time I came back to Damascus, appreciating my books, notebooks and other belongings, and all the photographs hanging on the walls. Every time I came home I opened my dresser and found that the clothes I had left behind no longer fitted. I had lost ten kilos in the past two years. In the dining room, my mother finished setting the table. She had prepared all the food that I had missed, and had chilled a bottle of the Chilean white wine she knew I liked. We sat in front of the television, chatting and eating and drinking, recovering a sense of family, the two of us, as we had done in the years after the death of my father, apparently now a wanted man.

Around midnight, my mother got up and went out of the living room, into the kitchen perhaps. She left her phone on the table. It rang. An unknown number.

—Hello?—*Good evening, madam.*—Hello, who's calling?—*You don't know me.*—Excuse me?—*Madam, why didn't you spend the Eid holiday with us? It's just not right.*—I don't understand.—*Eid's come and gone, madam, and you didn't spend it with us. We thought you knew where you came from, but it turns out you come from nothing.*—Who am I speaking to?—*I told you, you don't know me. Are you sitting down to dinner with your daughter? Did she just get back from Beirut? Is it nicer in Lebanon? What's for dinner tonight . . . ?*

I hung up. Panic swept over me, I felt light-headed.

I was suddenly short of breath, a wave of sweat poured down my whole body, and a tingling sensation spread down my neck to my chest, fingers and stomach. I shouted for Mama and told her, my voice wavering, that one of them was watching us; he might be standing at the door to our building ready to break into the house. I drew all the curtains, locked the door and went to my room. I took a whole Xanax. I lay down on the bed, hugged my knees, curled up in the foetal position. My body quivered like a slaughtered chicken. Every part of me was shaking. My teeth, eyes, hands, feet, stomach and heart shook; even my stomach was shuddering inside me.

My mother came in and hugged me and tried with all her strength to control my shaking. My body kept trembling for half an hour until it wore itself out, and the effects of the tablet began to flow through my veins. I stretched out, and my body began to relax. I cried feverishly. I couldn't sleep that night.

It was my last visit, and I didn't even know it.

The waiting room was still crowded when I left Kamil's office, and I asked Leila to walk me to the front door. There I asked if she'd be willing to meet me at a coffee shop nearby when she finished work. I told her I wanted to speak to her about something important. Leila agreed to come as long as we didn't stay late, because she wanted to get home.

I waited for her at a juice shop on al-Taliani Street, where the owner had expanded his shop by staking four tables on the pavement, which ate into the pedestrians' pathway. He'd also bought a little machine that made coffee to order. Al-Taliani Street was crowded. I saw a heavyset woman in her fifties lying down on the pavement, and noticed that she was wearing swimming goggles. She had a snorkel in her mouth, too, and was holding a phone to her ear. She was shouting into it, but it didn't seem like anyone was on the other end: she was at sea trying to rescue her son, she said, but so far she'd only found pieces of a wrecked boat.

None of the passers-by paid attention to what she was saying, nor did they laugh at the sight of her swimming on land. Not even the policeman standing there paid attention to the story of her drowned son, who had run away from death in Syria straight to death elsewhere. I thought of Naseem. Was this because the woman was wearing swimming goggles, breathing through a snorkel and talking about drowning? Or because he'd travelled to Germany the same way, with his traumatised, paralysed father? I had never asked how he managed to carry his father to the boat, and from the boat to the shore, from the shore to the Greek border, and from the Greek border to Germany. How did you manage that difficult route? How did you shoulder your burdens, and your father too, when you could hardly support your own body seething with panic?

Leila arrived, tired as usual, her face looking wan. She ordered a cup of coffee with milk, lit a cigarette and gazed blankly at the woman 'snorkelling', as if she were someone she saw in the waiting room every day. I sprung a question on her immediately: 'Leila, do you have a brother who's ill?' My question seemed to perplex her. She cocked her head and narrowed her eyes. Suddenly the tips of my fingers went cold, as if I'd plunged my hand into the same icy sea in which the woman was swimming.

'But you know about my brother!' she said. 'I've told

you about him several times, and you always ask how he's doing.' Then she offered a kind smile tinged with surprise. 'Have you lost your memory?' I felt confused; the narrow pavement transformed into a vast sea, and suddenly I was swimming too.

Had I lost myself in the story of the young woman in Naseem's book? I couldn't distinguish what I knew from what she knew any more. I'd mixed us up . . . I envisioned myself cradling her memories in my hands, and imagined her doing the same with mine. I had thought she was the one who knew about Leila's brother! Had I lost my memory and borrowed hers? Was I going mad? Had Kamil gone mad too, along with me, Leila, the woman snorkelling and searching for her son's body, and the policeman who was apathetic towards this drowning? Had Kamil's prophecy come true; had we lost our minds, all of us?

My voice wavered in my throat, my vision flickered. I thought my mind wouldn't rest until I met this unnamed woman who, like me, had lost her father; the woman whose story Naseem had stolen and penned . . . Naseem: a writer like the woman's father, a doctor like mine. The woman who embodied my stories so completely that for a moment I'd thought my experiences were hers.

I summoned the courage to ask Leila whether there was a woman, someone whose name I didn't know, who had seen Kamil regularly until three years ago, when she'd stopped coming back to Damascus. Leila looked lost in thought. I felt as if she were searching my eyes for some other detail.

'She's a writer in her thirties,' I told Leila, 'her father died when she was fourteen, she lives in Beirut now and suffers from panic attacks . . . and is fluent in French.'

Leila smiled. 'You know all this, but you don't know her name?' she asked.

I told her I'd run into the woman a couple of times in the waiting room, and once overheard Leila speaking with her in French. Another time I heard her mention her father in passing, when they were talking about Leila's father, who had also passed away. Elaborating on my lie, I added that I hadn't run into her for a while and missed her, and was worried about her disappearing, especially in these difficult times.

'You know her name is Salma?' Leila said with a smile. 'Salma. Suleima. Your name is a nickname for hers.'

Her words seemed to slap me. I felt my knees go slack. I heard her repeating the sentence again and again, without stopping. I was afraid. I couldn't make sense of my confusion in the moment, and Leila sensed the bewilderment streaming from me, onto the table at which we were sitting, pouring off it and flowing across the ground, all the way to the woman swimming on land in search of her son. I pulled what remained of me together and asked her why Salma had stopped seeing Kamil. Leila said that Salma was living in Beirut, working at a Lebanese publishing house and an NGO that served refugees. She was afraid of returning to Damascus because she was wanted by one of the security agencies.

What else did Leila say? She said she hadn't heard from Salma in two years. Salma used to call from time to time, until she didn't. Somehow words came then, and I told Leila that she didn't call because she was afraid of not being able to reach them at the office. Leila was silent; she clearly didn't feel the need to respond. Then I told her that I had plans to go to Beirut soon, that my work had been selected for an exhibition about Syria, and I wanted to invite Salma. I asked Leila for Salma's phone number. She said she didn't know her number, but she wrote down the name of the publishing house where she worked. I took the paper between my fingers and gripped it like a talisman.

I'd lied again. I had stopped painting in early 2012. I couldn't even bear to be in front of a canvas any more. I'd stand in front of the white, pick up a brush, submerge it in blue, and then find myself without the strength to lift it to the canvas. I could see a painting in that white space and so to use colours seemed futile. I felt that adding any colour to a white canvas would destroy it. I stopped drawing, too. The white canvas was still in my room, though the colour had changed; the fabric had faintly yellowed.

I decided I would go to Beirut.

Why hadn't Naseem ever written anything about Salma's work? Maybe it was missing because his novel was unfinished – but why hadn't he mentioned her name? Salma?

She had my proper name. She carried me in her soul, and I carried her in mine. Her name completed mine; just like Leila said, mine is a nickname for hers. She might even be carrying my memories and suffering with them, just as I've suffered with hers. I've dreamed of ridding myself of them all at once, as my father did.

Was Naseem's manuscript really about me? My name just happened to be similar to Salma's? But no – she is in Beirut, not Damascus. Her father was a writer, not a doctor. And she really exists!

I felt utterly lost. Naseem's manuscript was like a mirror: I read it and saw myself, nameless and without a home. Had he not thought my name was worth the trouble, and left me without an identity?

I called Naseem and left a voicemail, saying: 'I finished reading the manuscript you sent me.' If he listened to it, he didn't respond. I texted him and said I wanted to talk. He wrote back curtly: *Not in the mood*. I told him I was going to Beirut the following week. He didn't ask why, didn't say anything. Just silence, as usual. Even his silence was apathetic. It turned me into someone who belonged nowhere, someone entirely unmoored.

The next time I saw Kamil, I told him this wasn't just about madness, it was bigger than that.

'Not that long ago, you were afraid of going mad.

Now there's something bigger than madness?' he asked with a hint of irony, his lips stretching into his usual laconic smile.

I told him that what I was feeling was deeper than madness. I felt like I didn't exist, and it frightened me. I'd begun seeing everything through a lens of terror, and felt like nothing existed beyond my own body. I felt my mother wasn't there any more, like Fouad, who had disappeared, or my father, who had passed away, or Naseem. Or maybe they existed somewhere separate from me, and did not sense my existence. Eventually I lost my words, unable to express myself.

'I don't know if you understand,' I whispered to Kamil.

He smiled tenderly and nodded. 'If I understand . . . if I understand . . . Go on.'

I told him I was also afraid that I wasn't actually sitting in his office right now. I felt as though I didn't exist or belong anywhere, and it kept me up at night; I felt so alone, as if I were on the verge of death.

'The dead can't die,' said Kamil.

True, but it wasn't that I felt like I was dead, just that I didn't exist – or maybe that no one else exists, and that we're all just a figment of imagination. Then I saw tears streaming from my eyes. I say 'saw', because I didn't feel them falling, or even pooling in my eyes before they did. I was separate from my body; I saw its eyes fill with tears and I saw it cry.

I lit a cigarette and took a tissue from the box next to

me. I wiped my tears. Maybe the tears made my soul more porous, because next I told Kamil that I thought Naseem might be the reason I felt I didn't exist. How could I exist when I was with someone so absent, who didn't feel as if he existed himself? How could I feel my body when I was with someone who inhabited the margins of life, like a shadow or a ghost?

Kamil nodded, and a smile of hidden triumph traced its way across his lips, as if to say that all I needed to do was make the slightest effort and I could cross from the hidden to the seen. Yes, I knew. It was Naseem. Who else could it be? It had nothing to do with him leaving the country. Ever since he'd come into my life, fifteen years before, I hadn't existed and neither had he. Was he an illusion? Did this man with his bones, this man I loved, ever actually exist?

Then Kamil led me further, to the other shore, and reminded me that I had never loved Naseem. I loved someone else, someone I imagined; I sketched his features, chiselled his muscles and bones, exhaled a soul into the body and called him Naseem. The man I loved had only ever existed in my imagination.

No sooner had Kamil helped me cross to the other bank than I felt lost all over again. A strange feeling trembled in my ribcage: a heavy lightness that made my body feel parched, and at the same time as solid and fixed as a nail. Gravity intensified, as if it had just been discovered! Or as if it hadn't existed but had suddenly sprung into full force, to defend and entrench itself. I felt a weight pulling me to the ground; I felt my bottom sinking deeper and deeper into the brown leather sofa, and I couldn't move it at all.

I texted Naseem a classical poem that evening when I returned from seeing Kamil:

> *Oh in his love so cavernous*
> *I am revealed diaphanous*
> *I cannot help but speak his name*
> *Yet could not say he feels the same*
> *He thinks of us, and tears subside*
> *I think of him, my tears arise*
> *His face shines with benevolence*
> *And sees in mine no friendliness.*

I changed it slightly, but I don't think I altered the general feel. I changed the start of the fourth line from *'And can say'* to *'Yet could not say'*, replaced *'tears arise'* with *'tears subside'* in the fifth line and added *'no'* to the last line: *'And sees in mine no friendliness'*. I texted it to him. He read it. He said nothing for a few seconds, and then texted, *You transcribed the poem wrong!* I wrote back: *I didn't transcribe it, I memorised it!* Immediately he wrote, *Same thing. You memorised it wrong! . . .* followed by a long silence, punctuated by my rapid, jagged breaths. I saw the olive tree on the balcony where I had buried myself and remembered the obituaries in his desk drawer. My thoughts began to disintegrate ... and images of his other women appeared before me. Their eyes peered out of the photographs, staring into mine, and all I could think of was his sudden departure and how he had not asked me to go with him, then I heard the slapping sound he made as he struck himself, and finally I remembered my own hands, and I hugged my body in fear.

All my thoughts and memories started colliding with each other; I found it hard to breathe and began to sweat. Another panic attack, and the blind desire to be rid of everything, every experience I'd ever had, every thought, every image I'd seen, my name, her name, everything. My heart rate accelerated. I picked up my phone again and texted, *Are you still in touch with Salma?* Silence. I imagined him slapping his face. Then I could see that he was typing and typing, until I thought he might send me an excerpt from the novel; he kept writing for minutes, and then ... what? Nothing. Just silence. He didn't send a single word.

I went to the nightstand between my bed and the balcony, opened a drawer and took out a photograph of him. I stared at the face that still made my body tremble, and was rocked by the longing that welled up in me. His face lived inside me, and when it disappeared I lost my way. I gazed into his shining eyes, so vacant, cryptic and self-contained. His smile, tinged with uncertainty. I noticed that his smile was traced only on the left half of his lips. I placed my hand over the right side of his face, precisely at the midline. When I looked only at the left half I saw a smile, verdant and ripe, holding a whole world of happiness. Then I covered the left half of his face, and looked at the right side. There I saw a mix of sadness and indifference, and that scowl stitched between his brows. I covered the right side again. I was perplexed by the smile that unfurled with such difficulty, not even across his whole mouth, only the left side. As if it might retreat at any moment. An incomplete smile. Just half a smile.

I applied my paintbrush to his deceitful half-smile, desperately wanting to snatch it from his mouth and transport it onto canvas, where I could make that half-smile whole. But I couldn't. I'd lost my ability to paint. I'd spent my time writing instead. Was I emulating Naseem, who wrote in lieu of practising medicine? Who carried his soul in open palms, and found more space to express himself in writing than in treating patients in their last hours?

(He'd never dreamed of studying medicine, it was his mother who wanted her only son to be a doctor. So a doctor he became, though one lacking in courage and generosity, and in the end all he did was kill his mother, again and again, with his obituaries. When she died for real, he wasn't there, and didn't have the chance to save her. He once told me that in a practicum in his third year, or maybe his fourth, he collapsed on the floor in front of his fellow students while watching the professor open a cadaver's stomach with a scalpel. He told me that the stomach of the man in the morgue was a real stomach, that he felt the scalpel pierce the man's soft flesh and heard the sound of metal against that pliant mass. He smelled something, saw a flash of red, began to sweat and then fainted, prompting a round of teasing from his classmates. 'You'll never be a doctor.' Full stop. That's what the teaching doctor told him when he regained consciousness.)

I don't know when I fell asleep. The photograph was still in my hands, with its dull, extinguished eyes and incomplete smile.

In my dream we were sitting on the little living-room sofa and he had his arms around me. My feet were hanging off the edge of the sofa and a soft beam of light flicked towards them, with the tip of its tongue. I buried my head in Naseem's broad chest and breathed in the wet scent of rain. I told him that it was raining in the living room, and that we should build a roof before winter grew colder. He said nothing. I raised my head and saw only half of his face. That graceful beam of light had scrambled up my legs to his face and thrown the left side into darkness. I could only see the frowning half of his lips. I went to grab a handful of light from the left side of his face and to pull it back like a curtain. I could grasp it between my fingers, I swear. It felt moist and tender to the touch. I wrestled with it, trying to cast it aside, desiring the side of his mouth with the smile.

A terrible loneliness stretched through my chest, once I saw and understood the despondent side of his face.

'What are you doing?' he asked.

'I'm grabbing a handful of the light and trying to throw it back.'

'But you're hurting me.'

I stopped throwing it aside and rested my trembling fingers on my thighs.

'Why did you rip up my photo?' he asked. 'Why did you only keep the eyes?'

'Because the eyes are the mirror to the soul,' I said, as if I knew what he was talking about. 'And your eyes hold my soul.'

'My eyes hold your soul,' he repeated. 'And your eyes hold the other women's souls.'

I woke up in terror, with his photograph quivering in my hands.

★

The moments passed, and I waited for morning. When I left the house, my mother was sitting by herself on the sofa, probably still reading the same page. I hadn't the energy to check. It was 8.55 a.m. (My relationship with time had long been riddled with anxiety. I don't like quarter- and half-hours; I prefer whole hours, like nine, ten, eight.)

I took Fouad's car, a black Peugeot 206. It was Friday and the streets were practically empty. I parked in front of Naseem's building, and saw that the checkpoint nearby was empty, save one disgruntled officer. I thought of

Yasmine, Salma's friend, who fell in love with the officer manning the checkpoint in front of her grandmother's house in al-Mazraa.

I went into Naseem's house. I turned on all the lights, even though it was morning, and went into the little kitchen, heated up some water and made a small pot of coffee. When I pulled back the curtains on an impulse, a single beam of light entered, just like in my dream. I sat in the sofa's embrace, exactly where a few hours earlier, in my dream, I'd sat in Naseem's embrace. I smoked a cigarette and drank my coffee very slowly. That languor made me feel yet again as if I didn't exist, as if I had no control over myself. It was a sign. Had I taken half a tablet just now? At nine thirty in the morning? Wasn't that rather early? Did time mean anything? I took out a tablet and broke it with my teeth so I could swallow half of it, or maybe a bit more than half. (Xanax wasn't sold in pharmacies any more; it had become much harder to import things. Now pharmacies only stocked Pazolam, which had the same ingredients as Alprazolam, or Xanax, so the only difference between it and Xanax was that Pazolam tablets were round, not oval-shaped, and they were thicker and denser, so they weren't easy to break by hand. Pazolam also took longer to dissolve. With Xanax, I could put a tablet under my tongue, let it soften, then swallow some water, and it would rush through my bloodstream and flow up to my brain. Not with Pazolam. This meant I had to wait longer for it to take effect.)

I rested my head on the back of the sofa and closed my eyes. My longing for Naseem welled up; I felt my body hum with the desire to hold him and drink in his fresh, familiar scent. Then I got up and crept into his room. I opened the drawer and took out the photographs. I began ripping them up, one at a time, keeping only the women's eyes. Then I threw out all the scraps, and took just the eyes home with me. It was the first piece of art I'd painted in years, though it was not a painting in the strict sense of the word. I pasted the eyes next to each other in a collage on the yellowing canvas, one eye emerging from another. I took a picture and texted it to Naseem. He opened it. He spent a long time looking at it. Then, silence.

At my next appointment with Kamil, there were so many things I intended to tell him but didn't. I wanted to tell him that there were no men in my life any more, just like Salma. My father died young, Fouad disappeared, and Naseem left the country. I was left alone with my mother, just like Salma was left alone with hers. I wanted to ask him to open one of his chilled metal drawers and take out her file, and I wanted him to finish piecing me together again.

I wanted to ask him why Salma was free, while I was still confined to his office, to my qualms and pain, to this overwhelming grief that sought shelter in my soul, and in which my soul in turn took refuge. What little detail enabled her to orbit the space of her problems without turning to Kamil and asking him to hold her hand as she crossed from one bank to the other? Like me, was she in love with an imaginary man?

I didn't say any of this to Kamil . . . but I did emerge from his office all in one piece. Quite literally. My hands didn't feel separate from my body, and nor did my legs or my head or my hair. I was a single slab of being . . . so how could I walk? How could one piece of flesh move its feet or take a step? I don't remember how I got home. I just remember feeling viciously hot, enough to scald the sun itself. I took a bag of ice and a bottle of water from the freezer, lay down on my bed and put the bottle between my legs and the bag on my head. I rocked with tears as they streamed from my eyes. I didn't know whether I was shaking from the cold or from my tears . . . either way, it didn't matter.

I packed in a small bag everything I would need for two days. I told my mother that an art space in Beirut wanted to put on a show about Syria, and had invited me there to discuss the project and the possibility of me participating in a joint exhibition. My mother glanced at me without interest. 'An exhibition about Syria?' she said sarcastically. I didn't respond. What did she want? For me to pick up a weapon, go out into the streets and fight alongside the rest? And if I were killed, would my mother be able to handle losing her brother, husband, son – and daughter too? Was there room in her heart for more grief? I didn't respond. I kissed her on the forehead and left.

We passed through all the hastily erected checkpoints before the official border. I had my ID card, but didn't need to show it. I used my passport, which had been issued in Damascus. My father had wanted to change the residence on our family's official ID cards to Damascus, but it would have taken a miracle, given my mother's feelings on the matter. She said she'd put up with enough of his cowardice; she had abandoned her family in Hama to run away with him and their children, and this was the last straw. She made him choose between a Damascus ID and his marriage. And so officially, we were still residents of Hama.

I didn't show my ID. I looked directly at the officer as he stared at my passport for a long time. He flipped through it from right to left, and then back again. I don't know what he was looking for; I didn't have any visas, and with the exception of a few old stamps from trips to Beirut, the pages weren't marked. There were four of us in the shared taxi and he tossed our passports back at us all: a woman in her sixties, her twenty-something daughter, a young man in his thirties, and me.

It had been gravely silent the whole way from Damascus to the Lebanese border, but as soon as we crossed, conversation filled the little car. We were like statues that had just gained the ability to speak. The old woman peppered me with questions about why I was visiting Beirut, where I lived in Damascus, and current affairs. The man in his thirties sat next to the driver and joined the conversation too, commenting about his job in Beirut as a construction worker, and how he still couldn't bring his wife and kids to Lebanon. At one point the woman, who was veiled, said that she'd advised her daughter to stop wearing a headscarf. There were hardly any men in Damascus any more, she said; even clothing shops and corner stores were run by women.

We arrived at one in the afternoon. I hadn't been to Beirut in years. I asked the driver to take me to a hotel on Hamra Street, somewhere cheap but clean. The traffic was suffocating, and I had taken half a tablet before we reached the Syrian–Lebanese border. I took the other half as we descended the winding road, when Beirut appeared in the distance, draped in twilight and cloaked in mist, as if it were a dream, or as if I were. I felt fairly calm, despite the traffic and honking.

The driver parked near the entrance of a dreary-looking hotel, and told me it was clean and cheap. I got out of the car and entered with steady steps, arriving to meet myself. A young man greeted me and asked for my passport. He showed me the first floor where breakfast was served, and told me it started at six and ended at ten. He said that if I had any guests, they'd be required to show their ID for security purposes. He pointed out an old, dimly lit elevator. As the elevator rose, my heart began to gallop in my chest. I went up to my room on the third floor. Small, white walls, a balcony facing another building. Thick, heavy curtains were draped across the windows and balcony door, concealing the residents across the road from view. I went to the little bathroom and began filling the tub with warm water. I undressed and tossed my clothes aside, stepped in and let the water rise until it covered my shoulders and lapped at my chin. I let my body go limp. Being submerged up to my neck made me feel as though I couldn't breathe, so I eased myself gently up. I moved my hands around under the water, playing with the sense of space. Then I cried and cried.

I don't know how, but in that rare moment of relaxation, in a bathtub in a cheap, strange hotel in the middle of Beirut's crowded Hamra Street, my father appeared. Where did he come from, to gaze down at me so tenderly? I longed for another moment with him. Love filled each cell of my body, blossoming from every pore opening in the warm salty water. Maybe after advertising their proximity to the sea, hotels in Beirut felt obliged to fill their tanks with salt water? My father gazed down at me sitting submerged up to my chest. A desire raced through me to hug him, bury myself in his chest, return to him. This last part – the need to return – surprised me, as if he, and not my mother, had carried me inside him for nine whole months. As if I were still there, curled up in solitude. I missed going back to him and hiding within him; I don't know where exactly, but in him, inside him. Couldn't I sense his interior from the outside? Why not? I could hardly think of him without the need to feel his internal life.

He loved me. He really did. Of course, I know that every father loves his daughter, but he loved me more than average. My mother always said that from the time she was pregnant with Fouad, he had been waiting for me to be born. He'd wanted a daughter to name Suleima. My mother used to tease me, saying he would have been waiting for me even if she'd been pregnant dozens of times; even if she'd given birth to other daughters, he would still have been waiting for *me*! I didn't understand how he could have been waiting for someone he didn't know. He must have wanted a daughter, any daughter. My mother would look up, let out a sigh and say, with a degree of annoyance, 'No . . . no . . . he was *your* guardian. *Yours.*' I sensed a grudge behind her words. As if I were part of her long-standing disappointment in him. As if I had been his accomplice in the 'bitter times' she'd lived through with him.

I still don't truly understand what she meant by the phrase. I never saw him shout at her, begrudge her for snapping at him, get annoyed or complain . . . quite the contrary. I was impressed by his ability to bear her ever-present resentment, which steadily built to the point of shouted abuse. The most he ever reacted was by slipping away from the house to his clinic or a coffee shop. I never even heard him sigh or roll his eyes in front of her. He respected and loved her. He was aware of her anger, and absorbed her pain for her brother and family. He always praised her in front of their friends, and I once heard him tell them how he envied her rare courage and clear perspective. He said he would have been lost without those traits. I didn't understand what she meant by 'bitter times' or her 'tormented life' with him, as she described it on countless occasions.

(I miss him now more than I ever did before. Every time I think of Naseem, I miss him more. The more present Naseem feels, the further Baba recedes.)

My father wasn't handsome when I was a child, but he suddenly became handsome around the time I turned twenty. Of course, it wasn't that straightforward. He hadn't been handsome insofar as I hadn't paid attention to his looks. My mother dominated our view, my brother's and mine, always hovering around our father, so she was all we noticed. Fouad and I paid attention to her slender body, her lissomness, her fine posture and how effortlessly she held her head high, as if she had been born that way. We noticed her grace, and the brand-name clothes she bought from a high-end shop in Damascus that sold European imports. We paid attention to her leather shoes dyed in fashionable colours, and the short skirts that revealed her slender, stockinged legs.

We never noticed any details about my father, his clothing or shoes . . . until one day I discovered that he was handsome. He had attractive, sharply defined features. His eyes held a gentle magnanimity, as if his pupils were swimming in a still, calm lake. His hair was thick and soft, far from the style of the fifties or sixties. His clothing was youthful and sharp. He had a slender, almost svelte body. I realised that his allure was buried deep, under layers of worry as dense as bedrock. Yes. His charm wasn't forced, or even readily visible. It took effort to reveal this side of him, and my father didn't possess the strength to show himself as he was, not in the slightest, only how my mother wanted him to be.

When I realised this, I felt something like hatred towards her. I felt as if she'd kept me away from his real self, as if she'd squandered years in which I could have ladled him up, gulped him down and filled myself with him. I wouldn't have been left to love someone I could only imagine; my memory wouldn't need to borrow from others his features, the way he smelled, and the feel of his skin and bones beneath my fingers, in order to love him. I would have been able to release myself to a man whose every scent I knew, whose voice, whether timid or brave, was familiar. My mother kept me from him, and from having my fill of him.

This didn't mean I was left empty. He constantly brushed the walls of my soul, precisely because he was gone. Like my body was doing right now in this foreign bathtub. I submerged myself completely, and then all I had to do was lift my head and neck out of the water to feel him touching my shoulders. I don't know if I'm explaining this well. To miss my father, and to lament not having my fill of him, meant I missed myself in a way. In losing my father, I'd lost a piece of myself, for ever.

I sat in that little bathroom and cried and cried. I felt so lonely that I could hardly breathe, and the water started to feel like it was scalding my skin. I didn't know whether it was the salinity or sense of loss that burned. I got out of the tub and wrapped a towel around my body, then lit a cigarette and lay down on the narrow bed. I opened my purse and took out a small notebook.

I picked up the telephone receiver and dialled the numbers, just as Leila had written them a few days before. A man answered; from his voice it sounded like he was brushing fifty. I asked to speak with Salma. My heart was beating so intently it nearly leaped out of my ribcage. (Whenever my heart knocks in my chest like that and pounds with such determination, it feels like it is rising in my throat, about to choke me.) I would not forget the seconds that divided the man's voice calling Salma and her picking up the phone. Time moved slowly, as if this was eternity. Suddenly my fingers felt heavy, and the phone became a boulder in my hands, so arduous to hold up and press to my ear. I started swinging my feet in the air, to check whether time was progressing at its usual pace, not any slower. I moved them quickly and then became confused that they were going faster than my sense of time. My doubts about the nature of time intensified when I dropped the receiver, jumped out of bed to turn on the air conditioning, lowered the temperature to 16 degrees Celsius, and got back onto the bed. I gripped a cigarette between the fingers of my left hand and held the phone in my right. Either time really was moving slowly around me, or it was flowing slowly on the other bank, the one where Salma stood, and flowing past my own hands and feet at its usual speed.

Salma? Can you hear me? I'm at a hotel, I forget its name, halfway down Hamra Street, halfway down the street that runs from you to me. I'm standing on the edge as usual; I don't dare delve into the depths of things, I prefer the edges. Where I can be poised to escape. When I try to fall asleep in a big bed, I can't even shut my eyes, so I choose a spot closest to the edge. Falling off in the night is less frightening than being in the middle. At the theatre or cinema, I choose the seat next to the aisle; I don't like the front row because the doors lead directly there. When I'm in the car I sit next to the window, so I can open it easily and stick my head out to breathe. I always drive close to the hard shoulder, so that I can pull over whenever I want and get away. In recent years when I've needed petrol, I've asked our neighbour's son to take my car and fill it up, because of the queues at the petrol stations, long lines of stopped cars stuck one behind another, impossible to leave. What else? I hate snow because it hinders my movement, it makes it hard to get away . . . just like you at Dahr al-Baydar, when you were all snowed in and terrified you would die en masse. Six years ago, the streets in Damascus were closed due to snow, do you remember? I remember it so clearly; how I drew the curtains in my room, turned out the

228

lights, took a Xanax and hid under the covers, waiting for the snow to melt and the roads to open. I never lock the toilet door in restaurants or coffee shops. I keep a tight grip on the door handle so no one opens it, but I don't dare lock it, fearing I won't be able to open it again. Two months ago the electricity cut out, as usual, but this time I was in the elevator, and I banged on the door so hard I bloodied my hands. I was so afraid that no one would hear me and I'd die in that little box no bigger than a coffin. And now I'm talking to you, while sitting on the edge of the bed, in a room where the door isn't locked, where a little window looks out onto the street, which isn't blocked off, with just a thin towel wrapped around my body, cold air blowing out of the air conditioner, hitting my skin, dulling my pulse, yet even with all that, I'm not sure I could escape whenever I want.

Is that your voice? Do its reverberations make me feel more confined? Is it because you're waiting for me to respond? About who I am? I have learned that a person is more than her name, or the place she was born, or the family she belongs to. A person is her memory, all of it; how can I show you that? Where do I start? Putting dates in order and processing feelings aren't things that come easily to me. Can you still hear me? I'm Suleima. Who are you? When I'm at home and have a panic attack, I rush to my room like a madwoman, stand in front of the floor-length mirror and stare at my face. I look into my reflected eyes. I let my eyes brush across my mirror-mouth, and pass my fingers over the cold surface; I touch my nose and my cheeks, but don't feel anything on my face! It makes me afraid. That's me in the mirror, but I don't feel it. If I press a finger to my cheek in the mirror, there's no indentation. Fear dissipates gradually. I stare at myself as I appear on that smoothest surface. I use all my strength to make sure that I'm standing there, breathing. If I can see myself, it means I'm still alive.

Me, someone who fell in love with a man she invented and can no longer find. How do we come up with these dreams, and how can we lose them in the blink of an eye, sometimes without even realising? Is reality crueller than fantasy? Naseem conquered my fantasy of him, and then woke me up again. 'People are sleeping. If they died, they would realise it.' If I died I don't know if I would realise it. I'm sick with doubt about whether I really exist, or whether I simply invented myself, just like I invented Naseem and maybe even you, too. This has nothing to do with the deaths that Naseem planned out for us, the ones he carefully devised down to the last detail, from cause and manner of death to the funeral, the mourners, the myrtle and the acrid smell that accompanies the procession on one's final journey.

Wouldn't you think your story – my story – would be the last thing to make me feel I actually exist? When I read about you, I saw my feet walking to and from Kamil's office. I saw my persistent anxiety and dread. I found a sense of loneliness and of relinquishing everything beyond myself. Is there any sense in us meeting each other? Wouldn't that be like keeping a journal – the very thing Kamil advised me not to do?

If we do meet, it will be a dark and desolate act, a moment to recall our whole lives, yours and mine. I'll look into your eyes and see my own. I'll glimpse all the memories I still dream of giving up. I'll look into your fear, and see Naseem and his manuscript. I'll split a Xanax with you, and I won't ask how overwhelmed you feel, so as not to overwhelm you more. And you won't ask me. You won't be able to ask questions; fear gnaws deep into your soul and paralyses you. Do I carry you in my heart, will I carry you back to the city you love? Can I take you to Kamil, whom you don't dare call? Should I have brought your file with me from his frigid filing cabinet, as cold as a mortuary freezer? Or would mine have been enough for you to understand the fear that pours from my eyes? Do we share the same file? Should I tell you that Naseem didn't write you an obituary, or that he did, and that he gave it to you, and that you buried it in the dirt like I did?

We agreed to meet that evening at a coffee shop in Achrafieh. I told her that I was a Syrian painter in town from Damascus, that I'd written a novel and wanted her help finding a publisher. I intended to give her this novel as it stood, except for the ending, which I hadn't written yet. Time unspooled slowly. What would I do with my full heart and weary body? I looked in the square mirror across from the bed, and saw my run-down reflection. As much as I pitied the woman in the mirror, I missed her too. I wanted to bring her back, hold her tight against me and keep her for ever.

I remember now that every morning when Naseem woke up, he sat on the edge of the bed and then slowly got up, walked towards the mirror with anxiety-tinged steps, stood in front of it and looked at his reflection. He told me that every morning he feared not finding him-self in the mirror. He imagined standing there, looking at the smooth, cold surface and seeing nothing but emp-tiness. Once he fell asleep on the living-room sofa to avoid facing the mirror when morning came. He told me how terrified he was when he woke up the next morning, lying on his back with his right leg bent at the knee and his left foot raised, supported by the wall next to the sofa. Everything seemed mixed up. What was supporting what? Was the wall supporting his foot, or was his foot supporting the wall? Fear set in and he began to sweat, pressing his foot against the wall, afraid that if he gave up it would collapse on top of him. I forget if this was a dream he told me, or if this really happened.

I got dressed. Tied back my long hair. Beirut's humid-ity made me feel heavier, as if I'd gained weight. I searched through my things to be sure I hadn't forgotten my pack of cigarettes, bottle of Xanax, or the novel. I stepped into the small, suffocating elevator and took it down to the lobby. I asked the man at reception how to get to Achrafieh, and decided to call a taxi. I waited a few minutes and then went outside, got into a sleek car and told the driver the name of the café. There wasn't as much traffic as when I had first arrived. Car horns were no longer blaring . . . but I took half a tablet anyway to calm down. The driver stopped in the middle of Sassine Square and pointed his finger towards the coffee shop.

I got out of the car, feeling flustered and slightly dizzy. I walked slowly to postpone the moment of approaching the mirror – a mirror that would be neither smooth nor cold. I walked closer. Closer. The hands on my watch pointed to 7.30. The coffee shop faced the street and didn't seem crowded. I saw a young woman in her thirties sitting by herself. Her hair looked as if she had tied it up in a rush; there were a few loose strands. She gazed out into the street at cars and people walking by, and there was something like indifference in her eyes. She held a cigarette and was sipping a glass of white wine, or so it looked from far away. Was white wine her Xanax? Was her glass of wine like my half tablet, like the one I'd swallowed a few seconds earlier? Or did she not need it? Were we not reflections of each other in this way? I walked closer. Now she could see me. I stopped on the pavement with my purse in my hand, not looking directly at her so she wouldn't think that it was me. That I was her. That I was the one who called her today and asked to meet.

We were separated by such a short distance that her anxiety easily reached me. I didn't see it in her face, which had sharply etched features; it simmered in her eyes, I saw it swell, cascade at her feet and flow towards me. I wasn't sure whether her anxiety was what made me anxious too, because usually other people's composure is what heightens my anxiety. (Whenever I have a panic attack, I'm terrified by others' calm indifference. But nor am I comforted by their concern, or by their blank stares, eyes swimming with ignorance of what pains me. There's a thin line between indifference and anxiety, a tight rhythm. I need a precise kind of concern to calm me down. Few people can walk that line, few can throw me that line when I am adrift.)

It wasn't her anxiety that made me anxious, but the resemblance between our anxieties did make me stop. I stood in confusion at the edge of the pavement, catching my breath. Her anxiety was equal to mine, equivalent, it had the same look and smell. As if my own wasn't enough, I saw it before me and experienced it twice: once in my soul and once before my eyes. I felt it moan in my chest and watched it grow. It filled all my senses and then became weightless.

I wanted to close my eyes and leave, but I didn't know where to go. The need to flee rushed over me again, and I missed my father. I realised there was no one who could make me feel safe. My father was dead, Fouad had disappeared and Naseem had emigrated. I had no one left but my mother. I asked myself whether these men actually made me feel safer, or whether I imagined it. They had all disappeared suddenly. If my mother had been the one to disappear, would I instead have thought it was she who made me feel secure? Had I invented my anxiety? Or had I simply grown accustomed to it, from my very first breath? I could hardly think. I didn't know how much time had passed since Salma and I were supposed to have met. I saw her look at her phone, and imagined her checking the hour. I didn't sense that my lateness was what was making her anxious. A pervasive anxiety flowed through her body; it moved her heavy hands and drooping shoulders. A shadow was cast over her languid frame. That shadow's name was fear.

I stood there contemplating her, wondering whether my anxiety was a reflection of hers or vice versa, unable to take a single step past a line I'd drawn for myself at the edge of the pavement in the middle of Sassine Square. I felt sorry for her. She seemed lonely. And at that exact moment I was making her lonelier. But despite feeling bad for her, I also felt a desire to intensify her loneliness, for just a day. I thought about Kamil; if he were there he would say, 'You're only making yourself lonelier, not her. She's sitting in a coffee shop she probably knows, in a city where she's lived for four and a half years, waiting for someone she doesn't know, serenely smoking and sipping a glass of white wine. While you're standing there: a stranger, on a strange pavement, in a strange neighbourhood, in a city you don't know, as befits someone who wants to make another person feel more alone! Yes, you're the one who's alone here. All you have is the space your body takes up.'

I once told Kamil that I didn't understand my anxiety or my fear of fear. He asked me if I wanted to banish my fear for good. 'If I gave you a tablet to rid yourself of fear, would you take it?' I said yes. Kamil smiled, shook his head and clucked his tongue. He said that in one way or another, fear protected me. Fear wasn't just a defence mechanism I'd devised in order to survive in a place where I'd never felt I belonged. He said it urged me to live. If it wasn't for fear, I would have lost my impetus for life. I didn't understand. How could fear be my will to live?

Then he asked about my father. 'Was he overprotective of you?' I took a deep breath. I turned a specific memory over in my hands, one that felt both far away and imminently present. He wasn't overprotective, I said. He watched over me. He thought he was far enough that I wouldn't notice, but I noticed him clearly. He watched me while I ate. Sat next to me. He opened his mouth in the air when I opened mine, closed it over an imaginary bite of food, and chewed the air while I chewed my food. I hadn't stolen Salma's story in this, of course not. That's what my father did too. If Salma was her father's shadow, then my father was mine. He followed me through the house, in and out of every room, as if we were out for a stroll. He helped me with my homework. Worried when I was ill or came down with a fever. He never missed story time before bed. Kamil smiled. 'And then what happened?' He wasn't really waiting for an answer. 'He died,' I replied, and then said nothing after that. I didn't understand. Kamil raised his thick eyebrows. 'He died . . . and there's no one to watch over you any more. Is that what you're doing now? Are you taking on the task of watching over yourself, so that you can live?'

Yes. Practically all I do is watch over myself. I start the moment I open my eyes in the morning, by counting my breaths and monitoring my inhalations and exhalations. I feel sweat spread across my skin and take note of how cold it is, to distinguish between a panic attack and a heart attack. I hold a fingertip to the large vein in my neck to count my heartbeat. I perceive my interior as if it were the exterior, clearly visible. I sense every organ, one by one: stomach, intestines, oesophagus, larynx, lungs, bladder, liver. I feel faint movements inside me, and steel myself. I'm concerned about fear, and my excruciating efforts to examine my depths, to perceive the imperceptible. Breathing should be an unconscious act, and I've turned it into a conscious one, something I consciously observe and regulate.

★

I don't know what came over me! I started walking in the opposite direction. I rushed away from Salma like someone running from danger, from something in pursuit, like in the dream where the waves of the sea were chasing me and I was driving the car with myself, both of us ascending a hill towards a house perched at the top. Was that my dream or Salma's? I couldn't remember any more. I rushed away, towards nowhere. No home to return to now, no Naseem or Fouad or Father.

Suddenly I missed my mother. What was she doing? I wondered. Why hadn't I called her to let her know I was all right? Maybe I had assumed she wouldn't worry, or that she'd forgotten I'd gone to Beirut. Or that she wouldn't notice I was gone, immersed in her book, on page 24. It didn't matter. I missed her, and felt the desire to bury myself in the arms of the woman who had grown old in an instant, who thought she had lost her memory and mind. I walked quickly, and all the vitriol I'd felt that day vanished when I thought about her. (Or maybe it simply receded into itself, and could still stick its head out at any time?) At that precise moment, I felt that only my mother could soothe me and absorb the emptiness I felt when these men to whom I had belonged were gone. I walked until I was overcome by exhaustion, and then I stopped a taxi and went back to the hotel. It was just after 8.30 p.m. I packed my little bag with the few things I'd brought. I made sure I wasn't forgetting anything, and then decided to go straight back to Damascus.

I didn't want to wake up in this strange city; I didn't want to fall asleep far from my mother, my balcony and my little olive tree. I didn't want to fall asleep in a city my father hadn't died in, where my brother hadn't been abducted. Naseem's home was back in Damascus. I didn't have a home. But something was waiting for me there, and nothing was left for me here.

My mother was asleep in her bed. I kissed her. She opened her eyes. She wasn't startled by being woken by her daughter after midnight. Her daughter who had travelled to Beirut, intending to stay for several nights. My mother was her usual self: I didn't understand from where her deep sense of calm sprang. I told her I was home, and going to sleep. She smiled and shut her eyes, reassured. I slipped into bed.

I thought about telling her that I'd come home missing her more than ever. I also thought about killing her that night, the way Naseem had done. In this version I didn't ring the doorbell, so as not to wake her. I opened the door slowly and crept in on tiptoe, carrying my small bag so it wouldn't make a sound dragging on the tiles. I saw her sitting on the red sofa, reading. I went up to her. Her head was drooping and her body looked rigid. I shook her gently, but she didn't respond. I bent down to see her face. Her eyes were closed. A faint smile was traced across her mouth.

'Mama,' I called, the way Salma's mother had called her mother on that last farewell to her childhood home.

My mother didn't respond. I wrapped my arms around her, hugging her. Hadn't I come back from Beirut with an urgent need to embrace her? No: for her to hug me, not the other way around. How could she die and leave me, alone amid so much loss and grief? My body rocked with sobs, a moan of pain escaped my mouth, and my eyes were wet with tears. I felt lost in our little living room, suddenly transformed into a vast, borderless land. What could be harder than living without borders? Without a roof or walls? Anguished and abandoned, I wasn't strong enough to stand. How could I bury her myself? Where would I get the strength to live without her certainty about Fouad's fate? How could the days go on without page 24?

And then . . . I did none of this. I didn't have the energy to keep imagining such an awful situation. Didn't have enough air to survive without my fear of losing her. If she died, that fear would vanish too. And I would have no true fear with which to defend myself.

I woke to my mother's scream reverberating through every corner of the house. I got out of bed, terrified, and I swear my heart was beating so hard I could see my chest swell and recede, just as happened to Naseem when he slapped his face. I overcame my short, shallow breathing and ran. My mother was in the bathroom, screaming and wailing. I opened the door and found her standing with hands pressed to her cheeks, in a state of shock and fear. She saw me, and pointed to a hose next to the squat toilet. My mother had insisted that the guest bathroom should have a squat toilet, so she could use it too; she hated the idea of us sitting on a European-style toilet, and the traces of our bodies mixing with those of guests. The white hose had turned into meat! It was a deep blood-red, so fresh it glistened. I tried to scream too but my voice was trapped in my throat and chest. I tried and tried, but no sound emerged. I stretched my mouth as wide as I could, trying to let out a scream, but my voice hung there suspended, whipping in my throat, lashing me.

When I opened my eyes, I found my hand wrapped around my throat, sweat streaming from my body and my heart galloping. I took a breath to be sure I was able to scream and that I had my own voice, separate from my mother's. I got out of bed. It was quarter to seven. As I walked down the corridor I was suddenly overcome by loneliness. I could see my mother sipping her coffee, her book on the table in front of her. She noticed me. Turned halfway. Smiled at me. 'Coffee, sweetheart? It's hot.' And as for me . . . the smell of meat filled my nose; it rose up from my stomach and left a sharp, rusty taste behind. I smiled at her, and headed to the kitchen, taking care not to glance towards the guest bathroom, where the hose of living flesh was hanging.